REVULSION

Thomas Bernhard in San Salvador

Horacio Castellanos Moya

REVULSION
Thomas Bernhard in San Salvador

TRANSLATED FROM THE SPANISH
BY LEE KLEIN

A NEW DIRECTIONS PAPERBOOK ORIGINAL

Published by arrangement with Tusquets Editores, Barcelona.

Originally published in Spanish as *El asco:
Thomas Bernhard en San Salvador* by Tusquets Editores.

Manufactured in the United States of America
New Directions Books are printed on acid-free paper
First published as a New Directions Paperbook (NDP1344) in 2016

Library of Congress Cataloging-in-Publication Data
Names: Castellanos Moya, Horacio, 1957– author. |
Klein, Lee, 1972– translator.
Title: Revulsion : Thomas Bernhard in San Salvador /
by Horacio Castellanos-Moya ;
translated from the Spanish by Lee Klein.
Other titles: Asco. English
Description: First American paperback edition. |
New York : New Directions Books, 2016.
Identifiers: LCCN 2016003359 <tel:2016003359> |
ISBN 9780811223430 (alk. paper)
Subjects: LCSH: El Salvador—Civilization—20th century—Fiction.
Classification: LCC PQ7539.2.C34 A8313 2016 | DDC 863/.64—dc23
LC record available at https://lccn.loc.gov/2016003359

2 4 6 8 9 7 5 3 1

New Directions Books are published for James Laughlin
by New Directions Publishing Corporation
80 Eighth Avenue, New York 10011

Warning: Edgardo Vega, the central character of this report, exists. He lives in Montreal under another name, an Anglo-Saxon name that's not Thomas Bernhard. He surely relayed his opinions more emphatically and with more carnage than this text contains. I've softened perspectives that may have offended certain readers.

GLAD YOU COULD COME, Moya, I had my doubts that you would come, so many people in this city don't like this place, so many people don't like this place at all, Moya, which is why I wasn't sure you'd come, said Vega. I love coming here toward the end of the afternoon, sitting out here on the patio, sipping a couple of whiskeys, listening to the music I ask Tolín to put on, said Vega, I don't sit at the bar over there inside, it's hot at the bar, very hot over there inside, the patio's better, with a drink and the jazz Tolín puts on. It's the only place where I feel at peace in this country, the only decent place, the other bars are filthy, abominable, filled with guys who drink beer till they burst, I can't understand it, Moya, I can't understand how they so eagerly drink such nasty beer intended for animals, said Vega, it's only good for inducing diarrhea, what they drink here, and what's worse is they're proud to drink this nasty beer, they're capable of killing you if you tell them the beer they drink is nasty putrid water, but it's not beer, Moya, nowhere in the world would this seriously be considered beer, you know it as well as I do, it's a revolting liquid, but still they drink it with ignorant passion, said Vega, they are so passionate about their ignorance, Moya, they drink this nastiness with pride, even with a sort of national pride, they're proud thinking that they drink the best beer in the world,

1

they think El Salvador's Pilsener is the best beer in the world, not swill only good for inducing diarrhea as any healthy person would think, instead they say it's the best beer in the world, this is the primary and principal characteristic of ignorance, to consider your very own swamp water the best beer in the world, if you call it anything other than that, if you deride their swamp water, their nasty diarrhea-inducing swill, they're capable of killing you, said Vega. I like this place, Moya, it's nothing like those nasty bars where they sell that nasty beer they drink with such passion, this place has its own personality, it's decorated with some taste, although it's called La Lumbre, and it's horrific at night, it's unbearable with the racket of rock groups, the noise of rock groups, which is perversely annoying to all those in earshot thanks to rock groups. But at this time of day I like this bar, Moya, it's the only place where I can come, where no one bothers me, where no one hassles me, said Vega. That's why I invited you here, Moya, La Lumbre is the only place in San Salvador where I can drink and do nothing else for a couple of hours, between five and seven in the evening, for only a couple of hours, after seven this place becomes unbearable, it's the most unbearable place in existence thanks to rock groups, it's as unbearable as those bars filled with guys proudly drinking their nasty beer, said Vega, but now we can talk in peace, between five and seven no one will bother us. I've come to this place every evening since last week, Moya, I've come to La Lumbre every evening since I discovered it, between five and seven, which is why I decided to meet you here, I have to chat with you before I leave, I have to tell you what I think about all this nastiness, there's no one else I can relate my impressions to, the horrible thoughts I've had here, said Vega. Since I saw you at my mother's wake, I said to myself, Moya is the only person I am going to talk to, no other friends from school showed up at the funeral, no one else thought of me, none of the people who call themselves my friends showed up when my old mother died, only you, Moya, but maybe it's for the best, because none of my school friends were really my friends, none of them I saw after school ended, it's better that they didn't show up, better that none of my old companions showed up at my mother's wake, except you, Moya, because I hate wakes, I hate to receive condolences, I don't know what to say, it bothers me when these strangers come up to hug you and act like intimate acquaintances only because your mother has died, it'd be better if they didn't show up. I hate to have to be nice to people I don't know, and the majority of people who give you sympathy, the majority who help at the wake, are people you don't know, you'll never see them again in your life, Moya, but you have to put on a good face, a contrite and grateful face, a face that's truly grateful for these complete strangers who have come to your mother's wake to extend their condolences, as though in times like these what you most need is to be kind to strangers, said Vega. And when you arrived, I thought what a good guy Moya is, and it's even better that he left so quickly, good old

Moya, he left so promptly, I thought, I don't have to deal with any old school friends, said Vega, I don't have to be kind to anyone, because hardly anyone attended my mother's wake, except my brother Ivo and his family, a dozen acquaintances of my mother and my brother, and me, the oldest son, who had to come as quickly as he could from Montreal, who'd hoped to never return to this filthy city, said Vega. Our ex-friends from school have turned out for the worst, Moya, they're truly revolting; what luck I didn't run into any of them, except for you, of course, we have nothing in common with them, there isn't a thing that unites me with one of them. We're the exception. No one can maintain their lucidity after having studied eleven years with the Marist Brothers, no one can become the least bit thoughtful after enduring an education at the hands of the Marist Brothers, to have studied with the Marist Brothers is the worst thing that's happened to me in my life, Moya, to have studied under the orders of those fat homosexuals has been my worst shame, there is nothing as stupid as having graduated from the Liceo Salvadoreño, the Marist Brothers' private school in San Salvador, the best and most prestigious Marist Brother school in El Salvador, there's nothing as degrading as studying with the Marists who molded our spirits for some eleven years. That doesn't seem so long, Moya? Eleven years listening to idiocies, obeying idiocies, swallowing idiocies, repeating idiocies, said Vega. Eleven years responding yes, brother Pedro; yes, brother Beto; yes, brother Heliodoro, at the most revolting

4

school for submission of the spirit, that's what we were in, Moya, which is why I don't care if any of those characters who were our friends there came to my mother's wake, they underwent eleven years of spiritual domestication, eleven years of spiritual misery they wouldn't want to remember, eleven years of spiritual castration, whoever would have showed up would have served only to remind me of the worst years of my life, said Vega. But I just ordered a drink, as you can tell by my rant I haven't settled down, drink a whisky with me, let's call Tolín, the bartender, the disc jockey, the jack of all trades at this hour, he's a good guy, someone I'm grateful to for minimally easing my stay in this horrible country. It makes me happy to chat with you, Moya, although you've also studied at the Liceo like me, although you have the same uncleanliness of soul that the Marist Brothers instilled in me during those eleven years, I'm glad to have run into you, an ex-Marist student, who hasn't participated in the general cretinism, in this we're similar, Moya, you're the same as me, said Vega. I've been away from this country for eighteen years, and for eighteen years I haven't missed any of this, because I was precisely fleeing from this country, it seemed the cruelest and most inhuman thing that I was destined to be born in this place considering all the possible places in the world, I never could accept that of the hundreds of countries I could have been destined to be born in, I was born in the worst country of all, the stupidest, the most criminal, I could never accept it, Moya, which is why I went to Montreal well before the war began, I didn't leave as an exile, not in search of better economic conditions, I left because I never accepted the macabre joke of being destined to be born in this place, said Vega. After I arrived in Montreal, thousands of sinister idiots born in this country arrived, fleeing from the war, searching for better economic conditions, but I was in Montreal well before them, Moya, because I ran from neither war nor poverty, I didn't flee for the sake of politics, I simply left because I never accepted the idiocy of being Salvadoran, Moya, it always seemed to me the worst kind of idiocy to believe you cared about being Salvadoran, which is why I left, and I neither interfered with nor helped those guys who called themselves compatriots, I had nothing to do with them, I didn't want to remember anything about this nasty country, I left precisely to have nothing to do with them, which is why I always avoided them, they seemed to me a plague with their solidarity committees and all their stupidities. I never thought about returning. Moya, it always seemed like the worst nightmare to return to San Salvador, I always feared that the moment would come when I had to return to this country, and I avoided it by any means necessary, I avoided it at all costs, the possibility of returning to this country, and not being able to leave again was always my worst nightmare, I swear, Moya, this nightmare wouldn't let me sleep for years, until they gave me my Canadian passport, until they converted me into a Canadian citizen, until then this horrible nightmare ruined me, said Vega. I mustered the courage to come because of this,

Moya, because my Canadian passport is my guarantee, if I didn't have this Canadian passport I would have never been motivated to come, it never would have occurred to me to get on a plane if it weren't for my Canadian passport. Even so, I came because my mother died, Moya, the death of my mother is the only reason I felt obliged to return to this filthy pit, if my mother hadn't died I would never have returned, even when I was thinking that my mother would eventually die, Moya, it never occurred to me that I needed to come back. My brother had said he would arrange everything, he would sell my mother's belongings and wire my share of the inheritance to my bank account in Montreal, said Vega. I had no intention of coming even for my mother's wake, Moya, she knew it, every time she came to Montreal to visit me I repeated that I didn't plan to return if she died, that I wanted nothing to do with this filthy pit of corruption, and my mother always told me not to be such an ingrate, that when she died I had to return to attend her wake, she told me this so often, she insisted to such an extent, it weighed on me so negatively, that now I'm here. My mother won, Moya, she made me return; she's dead now, sure, but she won: after eighteen years I'm here, I returned for nothing other than to confirm that I did quite well by leaving, that the best that could have happened was to distance myself from this misery, that this country isn't worth it, this country is a hallucination, Moya, it only exists because of its crimes, as such it was smart to distance myself from this country, to change nationality, to not want to know anything about this place, it's the best that could have happened to me, said Vega. Here comes Tolín with your drink, Moya, it delights me to befriend whoever serves me drinks, I love that they serve me substantial drinks at this bar, without chintziness, without measuring, nothing more than tipping the bottle over the glass, which is why I like to come to this place, Tolín is an excellent bartender, he gives me the best service, he serves me the best drinks, if he weren't here I wouldn't come, don't doubt it, I come here because Tolín pours me generous whiskeys, said Vega. Thankfully I found this place to make my stay a little more tolerable, Moya, because in the end I had to return because of my mother: she avenged everything, the old lady, she avenged everything I did to her in Montreal, she avenged my disappearance, she listened to none of my negativity about this country, my outright negativity she countered with the whereabouts of Tweedledum and Tweedledee, she countered that one of my childhood friends has become a successful engineer and the other worked in an esteemed medical office, she retaliated after hearing me debase every single thing that had to do with this country, telling me about my school friends, my neighborhood friends, said Vega. The last time my mother came to Montreal twelve years ago, she warned me, Moya, she said I had to return when she died, I couldn't be an ingrate. Now here I am, even if it's only for a month, even if it's no more than thirty days, I don't intend to stay here a day longer, although we haven't been able to sell my mother's house; I'm here in a place I never thought I'd return to, to which I never wanted to return. But I don't understand what you're doing here, Moya, this is something I wanted to ask you, this worries me the most, how could someone who wasn't born here, someone who is free to live in another country, someplace minimally decent, prefer to stay in this shithole, explain it to me, said Vega. You were born in Tegucigalpa, Moya, you spent ten years during the war in Mexico, which is why I don't understand why you're here, how could it occur to you to return to live here in this shithole, to settle in a city that sucks you down more and more into its pit of filth. San Salvador is horrible, Moya, and the people who populate it are worse, they're a putrid race, the war unhinged everyone, and if it was already dreadful before I took off, if it was unbearable for my first eighteen years, now it's vomitous, Moya, a truly vomitous city where only truly sinister people can live, which is why I can't explain why you're here, how you can be around people who are so repulsive, around people whose greatest ambition in life is to be a sergeant; have you seen them walk, Moya? I can't believe it when I see it, it's the most repulsive thing, I swear, they all walk like they're soldiers, they cut their hair like they're soldiers, they think like they're soldiers, it's horrific, Moya, they all want to be in the military, they'd all be happy if they were in the military, they'd all love to be in the military so they'd have the power to kill with total impunity, everyone carries a desire to kill in their eyes, in the way they walk, the way they talk, they all want to be in the military so they can

9

kill, this is what it means to be Salvadoran, Moya, to want to be like a solider, said Vega. It's revolting, Moya, there's nothing that produces more revulsion in me than soldiers, as such I've suffered revulsion for fifteen days, it's the only thing this country produces in me, Moya, revulsion, a terrible, horrible, dreadful revulsion that everyone wants to be like soldiers, to be a solider is the best thing they can imagine, it's enough to make you vomit. Which is why I say I don't understand what you're doing here, although Tegucigalpa must be more horrible than San Salvador, the people in Tegucigalpa must be imbeciles just like the people in San Salvador, in the end they're two cities that are too close to each other, two cities where the military has dominated for decades, infected, horrid, filled with guys wanting to be in good standing with the military, wanting to be around the military, anxious to be like soldiers, they look for the least opportunity to grovel before the military, said Vega. It's truly revolting, Moya, the only thing I feel is a tremendous revulsion; I've never seen such a bottom-dwelling race, so fawning, so happy to whore themselves out to soldiers, I've never seen anyone so possessed and criminal, with all the vocation of an assassin, it's truly revolting. Just being here fifteen days has been enough to know I'm in the worst place: right now it's okay because there's no one here at the bar, Moya; I can assure you that after eight tonight, when the lunatics begin to come for the rock show, I can assure you, the majority will enter with a look in their eyes intending to make it clear they're capable of murdering you at the least provocation, for them the act of murdering you doesn't have the least importance, really they're hoping you give them the opportunity to demonstrate that they're capable of murdering you, said Vega. What beauties they are, Moya, if you think about it carefully, it makes you realize what a truly beautiful people they are, the only thing that's important to them is how much cash you have, they're not interested in anything else, they measure you by how much cash you have, there's no other value, and it's not that how much cash you have is above all other values, that's not what it means, Moya, it means that there's *no other* value, another value beyond this doesn't exist, clear and simple, it's the only value that exists. Which is why it makes me laugh that you're here, Moya, I don't understand how it could have occurred to you to come to this country, to return to this country, to settle here, it's truly absurd if you're interested in writing literature, this demonstrates that really you're not interested in writing literature, no one interested in literature could opt for a country as degenerate as this, where no one reads literature, where the few who *could* read, never read it; just to give you an idea, Moya, the Jesuits discontinued the literature major in the university because no one reads literature, no one's interested in literature here, which is why they discontinued the course of study, because there are no students of literature, all the kids want to study business administration, this is what interests them, not literature, in this country everyone wants to study business administration, in reality, in a few years, there won't be anything else but business administrators, a country whose every inhabitant will be a business administrator, this is the truth, the horrible truth, said Vega, no one's interested in literature, in history, or in anything that has to do with thinking or the humanities, which is why not one university offers a history major; it's an incredible country, Moya, no one studies history because there aren't any history courses, there's no history major because no one's interested in history, it's the truth, said Vega. And still the clueless of the world call this place a "nation," what nonsense, it's an idiocy that would be funny if it weren't grotesque: how can you call a place a "nation" if it's populated by individuals interested in neither general history nor anything about their own history, a place populated by those whose only interest is to imitate soldiers and business administrators, said Vega. It's totally revolting, Moya, total revulsion is what this country produces in me. And I've only been here fifteen days, dedicated to taking care of the formalities of selling my mother's house, fifteen days is enough to confirm that nothing's progressed here, nothing's changed, the civil war just served a group of politicians who made it about themselves, the hundred thousand dead are only a macabre by-product for a group of ambitious politicians who shared a shit sandwich, said Vega. Politicians stink everywhere, Moya, but in this country the politicians really stink, I can assure you that you've never seen politicians who stink worse than they do here; maybe it's because a hundred thousand cadavers expelled every one of those politicians from their murdered asses, maybe the blood of those hundred thousand cadavers makes the stench of the politicians here so unique, maybe the suffering of those hundred thousand dead impregnated the politicians with this particular way of stinking, said Vega. I've never seen politicians so ignorant, so savagely ignorant, so obviously illiterate, Moya, it's clear to anyone with the least bit of education that their ability to read has especially atrophied, once they open their mouths to speak you can tell it's been a long time since they exerted their ability to read, as such the worst thing that could happen to a politician would be to have to read aloud in public; I assure you that in this country there's no need to have a debate between candidates, it would be tremendous, Moya, it would be enough to ask the candidates to read whatever text aloud in public, I swear that only the smallest possible fraction of them would pass the test of reading aloud fluently in public. They bend over backward to appear on television, Moya, it's horrible, if you turn on the television at breakfast, on every channel there's an idiot asking the same idiotic questions to politicians who only respond with idiocies. It's only good for killing you a little bit, Moya, for forcing you to vomit your breakfast, for ruining your day. Television is already a plague; sure, in Montreal I don't have a television, but here at my brother's house, where I've stayed until this morning, they've forced me to watch television while eating meals; you wouldn't believe it, Moya, the television is in front of the dining table, it's horrible, you can't eat normally, you can't have any sort of normal meal, because the television's on ready to disturb your nerves. Which is why I've had to watch against my will and listen to these politicians reeking of the blood of the hundred thousand people they sent to their deaths thanks to their big ideas; these dismal types with their hands on the future of this country produce in me a tremendous revulsion, Moya, it doesn't matter if they're right-wing or left-wing, they're equally vomitous, equally corrupt, equally thieving, you can see in their faces how anxious they are to rob what they can; few of them really care, Moya, you only have to turn on the television to see in their ugly mugs how anxious they are to plunder whatever they can from everyone, these crooks in suits and ties that once had their feast of blood, their orgy of crimes, they dedicate themselves now to a feast, an orgy, of plundering, said Vega. But let's have a toast, Moya, we don't want to spoil our reunion thanks to these castrated politicians that each day ruin my meals, appearing on the television that my brother and his wife turn on the minute they sit down at the dining table. And the worst are these miserable politicians on the left, Moya, those who were once guerrillas, the so-called *comandantes*, those are the ones who produce in me the worst revulsion, I never thought they'd be such fakes, such lowlifes, so vile; they're truly revolting subjects, after sending so many people to death, after slaughtering so many innocent people, after tiring of repeating their idiocies they referred to as their ideals, now they act like voracious rats changed out of guerrilla military uniforms into suits and ties, they're rats that changed their spiels about justice for whatever crumbs fell from the tables of the rich, rats that only wanted to take control of the state so they could plunder it, truly revolting rats, Moya, it's a shame to think about all those imbeciles who died thanks to these rats, I feel sorry thinking about those thousands of imbeciles who were killed for following orders from those rats: those tens of thousands of imbeciles who enthusiastically went to their death following orders from those rats that now only think about acquiring the most possible money so they can seem like the rich they once fought, said Vega. Let's order another round of whiskeys, Moya, let's toast that it's still early, Tolín is on top of everything and serves us generous drinks; I'll ask him to put on the Concerto in B-flat Minor for piano and orchestra by Tchaikovsky, this evening I want to listen to Tchaikovsky's Concerto in B-flat Minor, which is why I brought my own CD with this stupendous concerto for piano and orchestra, which is why I came prepared with my favorite Tchaikovsky. Do you remember Olmedo, Moya, our friend from school, that idiot who always got excellent grades and tried to stay in good standing with the Marist Brothers? That really boring and undesirable guy who seemed like a priest thanks to his enormous desire to be in good standing with the priests? He was the only one in our class who went with the guerrillas, Moya, they told me about it a while ago, the only one from our class who died in the ranks of the guerrillas, that idiot Olmedo. You know what's even worse?

They executed their own comrades, executed them by firing squad in San Vicente, those rats who have become politicians ordered the execution, they executed him as a traitor, that cretin Olmedo, he's the only one from our class who died in the civil war, thanks to his imbecility, you could already see it forming at school, you remember, a guy who thanks to his naivety was executed by those rats, said Vega. They told me all about it recently: Olmedo was one of the hundreds of naive kids assassinated thanks to accusations that those rats were being infiltrated by the enemy, hundreds were assassinated by their own leaders who charged them with treason, they were assassinated by their own leaders' orders on the outskirts of the San Vicente volcano. Horrible, Moya, Olmedo was such a poor imbecile, he found the death he sought. It's horrible to think about the happiness with which some people kill in this country, the ease with which thousands go to their sacrifice like sheep for their vomitous causes, killed for their vomitous causes, ready to die for their vomitous causes, said Vega. And for what? So a party of thieves disguised as politicians can share the booty. It's incredible, Moya, really incredible, human stupidity has no limits, particularly in this country where people raise human stupidity to unusual heights, only in this way can one explain how the most popular politician in the past twenty years was a psychopathic criminal, only in this way can one explain how a psychopathic criminal who assassinated thousands in an anticommunist crusade transformed himself into the most popular politician, how a psychopathic criminal, who ordered the assassination of the archbishop of San Salvador, became the most charismatic politician, the most loved, not only by the rich but by the general population, it's a revolting, monstrous fact, if you think about it, Moya, a psychopathic criminal who assassinated the archbishop is transformed into a hero of the fatherland and transmuted into a statue paying homage to the people, because this torturer assassin blasphemed with such brutality that his tongue rotted with cancer, his throat rotted with cancer, his body rotted with cancer, only in this country and with these people could barbarism of such magnitude occur, it's so revolting that this psychopathic criminal could be transformed into a founding father, said Vega. Which is why, once I complete the sale of my mother's house, I'm leaving as soon as I can for Montreal, Moya, even if the house still hasn't sold, even if I have to leave the responsibility for the sale to my brother, to confide in him, even if in the end he deceives me and keeps my share of the sale of my mother's house, even if I lose the only inheritance my mother left me because my brother robs me of my share of the money, I prefer to leave as soon as possible, Moya, I cannot endure another minute, I could die of revulsion, of a profound and burning corrosion in my spirit, I will leave even if I have to before the sale; thinking about it, I could wait at most a week, but I don't have any reason to wait two weeks, tomorrow I'll change my reservation to immediately after the lawyer says I have to sign all the necessary papers, said Vega. I don't want anything to do with this country, Moya, other than to come here each day to have a couple of drinks at this bar between five and seven in the evening and sign the documents related to the house we inherited from my mother. I have nothing to do with this place. Listen to me closely, Moya, I'm sure that my brother will do everything possible to rob me of my share of the money from selling my mother's house, I've seen it coming from a long way away, he has every intention of taking the money from the house in Miramonte that my mother passed down to both of us, I could see from a long way away that he's worked with a lawyer to try to rob me of my small inheritance, because my brother Ivo never thought that my mother would include me in her will, he was always sure that my total absence from the country excluded me, and that he (Ivo) would be the only inheritor, he who would actually snatch the house in Miramonte, said Vega. Which is why Ivo must have been surprised when the notary read him the will that said that my mother had passed her house in Miramonte down to her two sons, with the only condition that I come to her funeral, after which he wrote me that it was up to me to decide what to do with this house. I'm completely sure, Moya, that if my brother Ivo had read the will by himself the moment my mother died, he wouldn't have alerted me, I'm entirely sure he would have invented something to keep me from coming here to claim my part of the inheritance, to get me to not fulfill the clause my mother included in her will. But Clara, Ivo's wife, unwisely called me minutes after my mother died, an unwise act that at the time seemed irrelevant to them, because they were both sure that I wouldn't return to the country, even if my mother was dead, but neither of them knew about the clause in the will that my mother had given to the notary, neither was aware that my mother had let me know already that if I weren't present at the funeral ceremonies, she wouldn't leave me any part of the Miramonte house, they both already believed they owned the Miramonte house, said Vega. And so it didn't shock Ivo and Clara when I announced that I would arrive the following day, when I asked them to delay my mother's burial until then, and when I entered the funeral parlor from the airport. Two days later the notary read us my mother's will in which she gave me rights over the Miramonte house, Moya, a house valued at one hundred thousand dollars because it's located just two blocks from the Camino Real Hotel, a house that my brother didn't have the least intention of selling because he wasn't desperate for the money, a house in which I lived practically my entire life in San Salvador, a house unrecognizable from the outside thanks to the cement wall surrounding it, a wall that never existed while I lived there, a wall that's not exclusive to my mother's house, Moya, because the terror everyone feels here has made them convert their homes into walled fortresses, a horrible landscape, Moya, this city of walled houses like barracks, each house is a little barrack the way each person is a little sergeant, both are evident, Moya, and now the enormous wall surrounding my mother's house is the best example,

Vega said. My brother Ivo couldn't believe what my mother put in her will, he also couldn't believe that I was interested in selling the walled house as soon as possible, anxious to rid myself of the walled house without the least delay, Moya, he couldn't believe the fact that I only wanted to secure some forty-five thousand dollars as quickly as possible, since I didn't have the least intention of returning to this country; for nothing in the world would I step foot here, this is what I told my brother and the lawyer, my only purpose is to sell the walled Miramonte house for money that will let me live more comfortably in Montreal and never again return to this revolting country, said Vega. My brother Ivo and I are the most different people you can imagine, Moya, we don't resemble each other in any way, we have not a single thing in common, no one would believe we're from the same mother, we're so different we never even became friends, only a few acquaintances know we share the same parents, the same last name, the same house, said Vega. We haven't seen each other for eighteen years. We never write each other. The half dozen times my mother would call me and he'd be with her, Moya, we'd hardly exchange hellos or commonplaces; we never called each other because we didn't have anything to say, each of us lived without having to think about the other, because we're complete strangers, we're total opposites, living proof that blood doesn't mean a thing, it's random, something perfectly worthless, said Vega. I just turned thirty-eight years old, Moya, same as you, I am four years older than my brother, and if my mother hadn't died I would have been able to live my entire life without returning to see my brother Ivo; that said, Moya, we don't hate each other, we're simply two planets on distinct orbits, without anything to say, with nothing to share, no similar tastes, the only thing that brought us together is the task of having inherited my mother's house in Miramonte, nothing more, said Vega. I have nothing in common with a guy who dedicates his life to making keys, a guy who has dedicated his life to making copies of keys, whose only concern is that his business produces more and more copies of keys, Moya, someone whose life revolves around a business called "Millions of Keys." His friends gave him the inevitable nickname "Key Ring," his total universe, his most vital worries, fail to exceed the dimensions of a key, said Vega. My brother is a lunatic, Moya, it causes me true sorrow that someone could live a life like that, it causes me profound sadness to think about someone dedicating his life to making the most possible copies of keys, said Vega. My brother is worse than someone possessed, Moya, he's the typical middle-class businessman trying to accumulate the money he needs to buy more cars, houses, and women than he needs; for my brother, the ideal world would be an immense locksmith operation, and he would be the only owner, an immense locksmith operation where they would only talk about keys, locks, doorknobs, latchkeys. And it's not going badly for him, Moya, on the contrary, it's going very well for my brother, every day he sells more keys, every day he opens another branch of "Millions of Keys," every day he accumulates more money thanks to his key business, my brother is a true success, Moya, he's found his goldmine, I doubt there exists another country where people have the same obsession for keys and locks, I don't think there exists another country where people so obsessively lock themselves in, which is why my brother is a success, because people need tons of keys and locks for the walled houses they live in, said Vega. For fifteen days I haven't had a conversation that's been worth it, Moya, for fifteen days these two have talked to me only about keys, locks, and doorknobs, and about the papers I should sign to make the sale of my mother's house possible, it's horrible, Moya, I have absolutely nothing to say to my brother, there isn't a single minimally decent topic we can address with intelligence, said Vega. The principal intellectual preoccupation of my brother is soccer, Moya, he can talk for hours and hours about teams and players, especially about his favorite team, called the Alliance, for my brother the Alliance is the finest manifestation of humanity, he doesn't miss a single game, he'd commit the most heinous sin if it meant the Alliance would win all its matches, said Vega. My brother's fanaticism for the Alliance is so high, after a few days it actually occurred to him to invite me to the stadium, can you imagine, Moya, he invited me to the stadium to support the Alliance in a difficult match against their longtime rivals, that's how he proposed it to me, as if he didn't know that I detest huge crowds, that concentrations of humanity produce in me an indescribable affliction. There's nothing more detestable to me than sports, Moya, nothing seems more boring and stupid than sports, most of all the National Soccer League, I don't understand how my brother could give a damn about twenty-two undernourished morons running after a ball, only someone like my brother could almost have a heart attack about the stumbling of twenty-two undernourished men running after a ball and making a show of their mental deficiency, only someone like my brother could have passionate ideas about locksmithing and a team of undernourished morons that calls itself the Alliance, said Vega. At first my brother thought he would be able to convince me that we shouldn't sell my mother's house, that it was best to rent it instead, according to him the real estate market improves every day, my brother said he had no desire to sell my mother's house; but I was emphatic from the start, I had no doubt that the best decision was to sell her house, it's what suits me best, so I never have to return to this country, so I can break all ties with this place, with the past, with my brother and his family, so I don't have to hear anything more about them, which, to be blunt, is why I was emphatic from the start, I didn't even let my brother make his case against the sale of the house, I said I only wanted my half, if he could pay me the forty-five thousand dollars right then, he could keep the house, that's what I told him, Moya, because I saw his intention to blackmail me with idiotic sentimentalities, with ideas natural to a guy whose life is limited to keys and locks, idiotic sentimentalities like saying my mother's house represents the family heritage, like saying we were raised there and similarly the house is associated with the best moments of our youth, I didn't let him continue with that nonsense, Moya, I told him that for me the family was coincidental, without any importance, proof of this was that the two of us had been able to pass eighteen years without a single conversation, proof was that if this house hadn't existed we surely wouldn't have decided to meet again, that's what I told him, Moya, and I explained that I wanted to forget everything that has to do with my youth spent in this country, my youth lived in this walled house that now I must sell, there is nothing so abominable as the years I spent here, nothing more repulsive than the first twenty years of my life, said Vega, they were years committed only to idiocies, Moya, horrible years, associated with the Marist Brothers, with anxiety about getting away from here, the uneasiness caused by the inevitability of having to live my life in the middle of this rottenness. I'll ask Tolín to play the CD of Tchaikovsky's Piano Concerto in B-flat Minor one more time, said Vega, I want to hear this concerto one more time before someone shows up with another request, I could listen to this concerto by Tchaikovsky a dozen times in a row without being bored, without being tired, Moya, I love this place because at this hour there are never other patrons who annoy me and Tolín always satisfies my musical tastes. Now I know that my brother will do everything possible to swindle half the money from my mother's house that belongs to me, now that he's realized I don't plan to return to this country, my brother will do everything possible to swindle the money from me, I'm sure, Moya, from miles away you can see his happiness about my decision not to return to the country, his expression reveals that he's thinking about the best way to maximize the selling price of my mother's house, he's thinking about the best way to avoid sending me the money that belongs to me from the sale of my mother's house, at the very least he'll delay sending it for six months so it earns interest sitting in his bank, said Vega. But this plan of his runs into one problem, Moya, a single, convincing problem, I've already revealed it by alerting the lawyer that if they try to perform any sort of fraud, I won't return to Montreal, instead I will waste my forty-five thousand dollars by making their lives impossible, they'll be confronting a Canadian citizen, so they better be careful. You should have seen the face my brother made, Moya, super-offended, as if I'd doubted the Virgin Mary's purity, said Vega, as if the ability to rob and defraud didn't precisely characterize the people of this country. My brother Ivo started shouting that I was disgraceful and inconsiderate with neither heart nor soul, I had scum in my head, and because I was like that, I thought everyone in the world was like me; he started shouting in the lawyer's office this morning that I didn't deserve anything, that he didn't understand why my mother decided to include me in her will when I had never worried about what happened to the family in my life. He was shouting at me like that, Moya, said Vega. And since my nerves were already shot after fifteen days in this country, after fifteen days in my brother's house, fifteen days of signing documents and visiting offices, as though my nerves weren't already disturbed enough I told him I didn't care what he thought about me, that if there were really something I didn't care about it's his opinion of me, that I'd never worry about the opinion of someone who only has his mind on keys and locks and, worse, intends to strip me of money by selling my mother's house, which is what I said to him, Moya, and I warned him that he couldn't defraud me, that he'd have to pay every dollar coming to me from the sale of my mother's house, said Vega. My brother is truly revolting, Moya, which is why I decided this morning to get away from his house, I decided to move to the Terraza Hotel this very morning, after leaving the lawyer's office, I went to my brother's house to recover my things and move to the Terraza Hotel, it's what I should have done as soon as I came to this country, I don't know how it could have occurred to me to accept my brother's offer to stay at his house, with his wife and their two kids, I don't know how the idea could have crossed my mind that I could stand living a month with people like that, only in a state of extreme perturbation could I accept the proposal to stay in my brother's house, Moya, taking into account that I've lived alone the last eighteen years of my life, taking into account that since I managed to escape this country and my mother's house I've always lived alone, said Vega. Luckily, Clara, my brother's wife, wasn't around when I recovered my things, lucky for her, I say, Moya, because thanks to my disturbed nerves I would have told her that I actually had nothing ingratiating to say to her, that the last fifteen days I spent in her house had been the worst fifteen days I could remember in my life, that I've never been immersed in an environment as miserable, as stupid, as foreign to my spirit, an environment that only served to keep me in a state of extremely anxiety, said Vega, everything was completely crude, the proper environment of a middle-class family in San Salvador, something I wouldn't wish upon anyone. My brother's house is located in Escalon Norte, Moya, a horrible neighborhood beginning with its name, a neighborhood for middle-class arrivistes aspiring to live in the actual neighborhood of Escalon but who don't have the money to buy a house in actual Escalon, so Escalon Norte was invented for these middle-class arrivistes like my brother, who as soon as they save enough money will buy themselves a house in Escalon, not in Escalon Norte that only has in common with actual Escalon the fact that both neighborhoods are built on the hillside leading up to the volcano, said Vega. It's horrible how this city has grown, Moya, it's already eaten up half the volcano, it has already eaten up nearly half the surrounding green area, people here have the tremendous vocation of termites, they consume everything, one only needs to travel a couple of kilometers from San Salvador to realize that sooner or later this whole country will be an immense filthy city surrounded by equally filthy desert, said Vega, the city as it is right now is one of the filthiest and most hostile cities, a city designed for animals, not human beings, a city that converted its historical center into a garbage dump, because since no one was interested in history, they figured the historical center was disposable and therefore they converted it into a garbage dump, really a citywide dump; it's a revolting city, Moya, intended for dimwits and thieves, whose only preoccupation is to destroy whatever architecture minimally suggests the past in order to construct Esso gas stations and hamburger joints and pizzerias. Tremendous, Moya, said Vega, San Salvador is a grotesque, inane, stupid version of Los Angeles, populated by idiots who only want to seem like the idiots of Los Angeles, it's a city demonstrating the congenital hypocrisy of its people, the hypocrisy they carry in their most intimate souls is that they want to become gringos, Moya, what they most desire is to become gringos, I swear, but they don't accept that their most precious desire is to become gringos, because they're hypocrites, Moya, and they're capable of killing you if you criticize their revolting Pilsener, their revolting pupusas, their revolting San Salvador, their revolting country, they're capable of killing you without blinking an eye, and yet they're absolutely not interested in anything other than destroying their city and their country with infectious enthusiasm. It's truly revolting, Moya, I assure you, I can't stand this city, said Vega, it has all the miseries and filth of big cities and none of the virtues, all of the negatives of big cities and not a single basic positive, it's a city in which you're screwed if you don't have a car, because the public transportation is the most incredible thing that can be imagined, the buses are designed to transport livestock, not human beings, people are treated like animals and no one protests, their daily life is spent treated like animals, the only way they're actually used to traveling by bus is if they're being treated like animals. It's incredible, Moya, the bus drivers have been pathological criminals since birth, criminals converted into salaried bus drivers, said Vega, they're guys who were no doubt torturers and participated in massacres during the civil war and now they're recycled as bus drivers; the moment you arrive here, to get on a bus is to realize you've put your life in the hands of a criminal who drives as fast as possible, who doesn't respect stop signs or red lights or any sort of traffic signals, a lunatic whose sole goal is to end up with the highest number of lives in his hands in the shortest possible time, said Vega. It's terrifying, Moya, an experience that's not recommended for cardiac patients; no one in their right mind could travel every day on a bus in this city, one would have to be permanently and sadistically degraded in spirit to travel every day with these recycled criminals who drive the buses, I swear to you, Moya, I made two trips by bus, soon after I arrived in this city, and it was enough for me to understand that repeating the experience would wreck my nerves in a flash, it was enough for me to understand the level of degradation bus drivers subject the majority of the city to on a daily basis, said Vega. You, Moya, because you have a car, you don't know what I'm saying, surely you've never needed to travel by bus, it never would occur to you to get on a bus, even if your car were broken down it would never occur to you to get on a bus, you would prefer to pay for a taxi or ask some friend to drive you where you want to go. The people in this city are divided into those who have a car and those who travel by bus, this is the most emphatic division, the most radical, said Vega, your income level or the area where you live doesn't matter much, what is important is if you have a car or travel by bus, it's truly an infamy, Moya. Luckily, now that I'm at the Terraza Hotel I won't need to deal with my brother anymore, or his wife, Clara, or their offspring, those boys that don't do anything except watch television, it's really incredible, Moya, that pair of kids spending their lives in front of the television, because I want to make it clear that my brother has three televisions in his house, you wouldn't believe it, three televisions they often turn on at the same time to different channels, a true hell this place is, Moya, I'm thankful to have left that house of lunatics this morning, they only spend their time watching television: the one television that mortifies me most is in the dining room in front of the table, it's situated in such a way that there's no way to avoid it at dinner time when you're trying to eat; the other television is in the kids' room, and the largest, with a gigantic screen and a VCR, is in the master bedroom. It's horrible, Moya, hair-raising if you think about it; a family that in its free moments at home doesn't do anything except watch television, said Vega, not a single book exists there, my brother doesn't have a single book in his house, not even a reproduction of a painting, not even a recording of serious music, nothing that has anything to do with art or good taste can be found in this house, nothing that has anything to do with cultivating the spirit, nothing that has anything to do with the development of intelligence, it's incredible, on the walls they hang only diplomas and stupid family photos, and on their bookshelves, instead of books, there are only those idiotic little trinkets that they search out whenever there's a sale of knockoff jewelry, said Vega. Really I don't know how I could have lasted fifteen days at that place, Moya, I don't know how I could have lasted fifteen nights in a row in a house where three televisions simultaneously droned, where not a single record exists with minimally decent music, we're not talking about classical, but minimally decent music, Moya, it's abominable the musical taste of these two, it's abominable their total absence of taste in everything having to do with art or any manifestation of the spirit, said Vega, they only listen to revolting music, tacky, sentimental music interpreted by singers warbling out of tune from beginning to end, and still my brother had the gall to ask me why I wasn't going to return to live in this country, it's incredible, Moya, that the possibility that I could return to live in this country even occurred to him at any point. I almost vomited, Moya, I almost vomited from revulsion when he said that, since I'm an art history professor and nowhere in this country do they teach art history, maybe I would have many opportunities to teach art history here, he said this to me, Moya, he said it seriously, that if I stayed in San Salvador I would probably become a highly coveted professor because there would be no competition in teaching art history, all the jobs would be mine: the universities would fight over me to be their top art-history professor, and maybe in a few months I would be able to establish my own art-history academy and then, why not, in a little while I could found my own university specializing in art. This is what he said to me, Moya, without laughing, I assure you that he wasn't making fun of me; he was talking seriously, lamenting that in the business of keys and locks there already exists sufficient competition, unlike in art history where the road is wide open for me. Luckily I've left that house, Moya, I feel as if I've rid myself of a weight on my shoulders, you don't know how good it feels not to have to talk with my brother and his wife anymore; but I want to tell you that my brother and his wife aren't the exception, Moya, imbecility isn't an attribute exclusive to them, some of their friends are even worse, I assure you, like this gynecologist to whom the brilliant idea also occurred that I should found a university of art; he's a gynecologist who evidently already has his own university, where they don't teach gynecology but business administration and other similar careers, a gynecologist in whose hands I wouldn't want to be if I were a woman, said Vega. Doctors are the most corrupt people I have encountered in this country, Moya, they're so corrupt that you cannot feel anything less than indignation and revulsion for them, in no other country are doctors so corrupt, so capable of killing you while stealing as much of your money as possible, Moya, doctors in this country are the most immoral people that exist, I speak from my own experience, no one is more appalling, more vomitous than this country's doctors, I have never seen anyone more savage and ravenous than the doctors here, said Vega. A week ago I had an appointment at which I was prescribed something for the nervous colitis that had been exacerbated by my mother's death, by my stay in this country, by staying at my brother's house, this colitis that's been with me ever since I can remember, Moya, but which is exacerbated when I am forced to confront disagreeable situations, colitis for which I only need some medication, but the doctor figured he'd encountered a gold mine that day, his eyes shone like you can't imagine, Moya, the most unbridled greed sparkled in his eyes; he couldn't hide his enthusiasm at having encountered a sucker to exploit in the most merciless way, it's incredible, a doctor here in a white coat with his hands recently washed is evil incarnate. He asked me to submit to thousands of examinations, making a face of compunction, as if my case were very grave, he said without the least reserve that I was about to suffer a peritonitis, and in the middle of his rehashed terminology he said that probably if the examination results were positive I'd need to consider the possibility of surgical intervention, he told me this, Moya.

33

You can imagine that I didn't return for another consulta-
tion, said Vega, that I just limited myself to taking a stronger
dose of my regular medication. Which is why I said who
knows what type of gynecologist this friend of my brother
was really, who knows how many women he disgraced, how
many children died thanks to his imbecility, he had to have
been a miserable gynecologist if it occurred to him to found
a university instead of simply working in his office, said
Vega, although in this country, founding a university seems
as easy as opening a doctor's office; I don't believe there exists anywhere else where there are so many private universities, the most private universities per square kilometer,
the largest quantity of private universities per inhabitant,
it's incredible, Moya, that just here in San Salvador there are
more than forty private universities, you can imagine, a city
with hardly a million and a half inhabitants has almost fifty
private universities, it's truly an aberration, because almost
all of these universities aren't anything more than busi-
nesses to defraud incautious people, it's the denial itself of
knowledge, take for example that in no other country is
higher education so thoroughly demolished at a level as low
as this, said Vega. The more private the university, the more
imbecility and treachery there is among those graduating:
that is the rule, Moya, clear evidence that knowledge interests no one in this country, people are only interested in
having a degree, obtaining their degree is the goal, to get a
degree in business administration that lands them a job, al-

though they understand nothing; they're not interested in learning anything, there's no one to teach them anything, the professors are a bunch of starving cats who were only interested in obtaining their degree so they could give classes to the next bunch of cats hoping to obtain their degree, it's truly a calamity, Moya, said Vega. And the most calamitous of all, what's a tremendous disgrace, is the University of El Salvador, the autonomous university, the only university maintained by the state, the supposedly governing principle of higher education, the oldest and at one time (various decades ago) the most prestigious university in the country. I couldn't believe it, Moya, the morning I decided to visit the campus of the University of El Salvador, I couldn't imagine anything so disgraceful, it seemed like a refugee camp in Africa: crumbling buildings, a ton of overcrowded, infested wooden constructions, and defecation in the hallways of buildings that were still standing, *human defecation* in the University of El Salvador's hallways, a fetid, revolting environment in the hallways of the country's main university thanks to human defecation that must be carefully avoided. Moya, the library is more suited for a kindergarten on the outskirts of some other decent city, a library in which are found only Soviet manuals, it's a university in which the few humanities and social sciences still taught are taught from Soviet manuals. I couldn't believe it, Moya, this university is a defecation, the University of El Salvador is nothing more than a defecation expelled from the rectum of the military and the communists, the military and communists allied in their war to convert the University of El Salvador into a pile of crap: the military, with its criminal interventions, and the communists, with their congenital stupidity, conspired to convert the oldest center of study in this country into a fetid and revolting defecation, said Vega. My brother must be an imbecile of the highest stripe to think I'd be willing to leave my chair of the art history department at McGill University to give classes at a corrupt kindergarten calling itself a university instead of a defecation maintained by state funds, he must be an utter imbecile to think I'd be willing to leave my chair to come teach a herd of cattle interested only in getting a degree in business administration. You'd have to be crazy, definitively, like yourself, Moya, to believe that you can change anything in this country, to believe it's worth it, to believe that the people are interested in changing anything, said Vega, not even eleven years of civil war served to alter anything, eleven years of slaughter and the same rich people remain, the same politicians, the same fucked plebes, the same imbecility permeating everything. It's all a hallucination, Moya, you understand: the people who think for themselves, who are interested in knowledge, the people dedicated to science and the arts, should get away as fast as they can from this country. Here you'll rot, Moya, I don't know what you're trying to do, your idea of starting a new kind of newspaper is truly naive, a stupid idea of feverish brains like yours that refuse to see reality. The people of this country

36

are fighting against knowledge and intellectual curiosity, Moya, I'm completely sure that this country is out of sync with time and the world, it only existed when it was a bloodbath, it only existed thanks to the thousands who were assassinated, thanks to the criminal capacity of the military and the communists, beyond this criminal capacity, the people of this country have no possibility of demonstrating their existence in the world, said Vega. The newspapers are precisely the best evidence of the intellectual and spiritual misery of the people in this country, Moya, until you leaf through the two morning newspapers you can't understand what country you're in; to understand the intellectual and spiritual misery of those who create and buy these newspapers, you have to understand that these newspapers aren't made to be read but to be leafed through, because no one in this country is interested in reading, and because there aren't people at the newspapers capable of writing readable articles, it's actually not about *newspapers* in the strict sense of the word, no one with the least bit of education would call these catalogs *newspapers*, these collections of special offers, which is why I say that people don't buy them to read them but to leaf through the ads, to be aware of the best offers, it's the only thing that interests people in these newspapers, the special offers and the ads, the only thing they're good for, the newspapers, are to help people stay on top of the special offers and advertisements, said Vega. And I've never seen such fanatical editorial writers, writers so rabid and obtuse, with the same intellectual and spiritual misery of the newspapers: this very morning one of the editors wrote that Bill Clinton is a communist, that the secretary general of the UN is a communist, that the UN is really controlled behind the scenes by communists. It doesn't matter that it's been four years since the communists left in a stampede, it doesn't matter that it's the President of the United States; for the editorial writer of these nasty catalogs containing special offers, time hasn't elapsed, and the world only revolves around his pathological obsessions, said Vega. They are truly revolting newspapers, if you think about it, Moya, but people like them, these people are so brute, so abject, that this is the type of newspaper they like, nothing can be done about it, Moya, which is why it's better not to stick your oar in these waters, it's better not to think you can change people's tastes with a newspaper you expect them to read, I assure you, no one will buy it, I assure you no one will be interested in a newspaper that's supposed to be read, it would be the strangest thing for a newspaper to exist in this country that's supposed to be read, people here are only interested in ads and special offers, said Vega. Luckily I'm only spending one more week in this pit and then I will be able to avoid shocking my nerves with these rabid catalogs they call newspapers here; luckily I no longer have to endure my brother and his family, Moya, luckily I can now lock myself in my hotel to read my books, to wait for the call from the lawyer to sign the last documents to complete the sale of my mother's house. You can't imagine the relief I feel knowing that

I'll spend tonight in my hotel room, Moya, said Vega, I feel an enormous relief knowing that the week I have left here, I can spend locked away in my hotel room with the air conditioner on, without having to accompany my brother and his wife on all sorts of horrible outings that they insist I go on, to all these horrible places that supposedly Salvadorans returning home are so anxious to visit, these places they call "typical" that theoretically I should have missed during my eighteen years abroad, as if I ever felt nostalgic for anything related to this country, as if this country had anything worthwhile for which someone like me could feel nostalgia. It's stupid, Moya, a tremendous stupidity, said Vega, but they didn't believe me when I told them that none of it interested me, they thought I was joking when I repeated that I hadn't been nostalgic for anything, and they schemed to take me out to eat pupusas in Balboa Park, to do nothing more than eat these horrible fatty tortillas stuffed with chicharrón they call *pupusas*, as if they produced in me anything other than diarrhea, as if I could enjoy such fatty diarrhea-inducing food, as if I would want to have in my mouth the truly revolting taste of pupusas, Moya, there's nothing fattier, more harmful for your health than pupusas, nothing filthier and more detrimental to the stomach than pupusas, said Vega. Only hunger and congenital stupidity can explain why human beings here eat something as repugnant as pupusas with such relish, only hunger and ignorance explain why these people consider pupusas the national dish, Moya, listen to me closely, never let it occur to you to criticize pupusas, never let it occur to you to say they're dealing with a repugnant and harmful food, they'll kill you, Moya, keep in mind the tens of thousands of Salvadorans living in the United States always dreaming about their repugnant pupusas, so ardently desiring their diarrhea-inducing pupusas that now there exist *pupuseria* chains in Los Angeles, said Vega; never forget that five million Salvadorans still in El Salvador religiously eat their plate of repugnant pupusas on Sunday afternoons, those fatty tortillas stuffed with chicharrón, this nasty greasy homecooked meal they serve like the host on Vespers communion. The fact that pupusas are the national dish of El Salvador shows that these people have dull palates, Moya, only someone with a totally dull palate would consider those repugnant fatty tortillas stuffed with chicharrón somehow edible, said Vega, someone like me with a healthy palate must endlessly refuse to eat such greasy nastiness, I once refused in such a way that my brother suddenly understood I wasn't joking, I wasn't going to eat those repugnant pupusas and perhaps this was the first altercation we had, in Balboa Park he began to reproach my ingratitude and what he called my lack of patriotism. You can imagine, Moya, as if I considered patriotism a virtue, as if I weren't completely sure that patriotism is one of many stupidities invented by politicians, as if patriotism had anything to do with these fatty tortillas stuffed with chicharrón that always destroy my intestines, that exacerbate my nervous colitis, said Vega. These were the outings with my brother and his family, Moya, a true nightmare, a way to exacerbate my nervous colitis, an effective way to disturb my nerves, there was nothing more destructive for my emotional equilibrium than these outings with my brother and his family, Moya, especially because my brother's sons have all the necessary characteristics to finish off my tranquility, just remembering that pair of kids can unhinge me, a pair of kids particularly stupid and pernicious because they don't do anything other than watch television, boys who don't have anything in their heads other than the television series they watch every day, for whom life is nothing more than a television series, it's truly horrible, Moya, I don't know how I tolerated them for so long without losing my temper, I don't know how I was able to withstand these stupid, pernicious boys for fifteen days, who disturbed my mood the moment they called me "uncle," said Vega. No single living human being seems more intolerable than these boys, Moya, there's nothing more unendurable than being with them, which is why it would never occur to me to live where there are children, said Vega, only the extreme state of my disturbed nerves produced by returning to this country explains why I accepted my brother's invitation to live in his house during my monthlong stay, knowing that my brother had two boys who are nine and seven years old, two boys more irritating than any children I have ever known in my life, because for my brother's sons I am not just any adult, for my brother's sons I am Uncle Eddie, what an honor, Moya, my brother's sons call me Uncle Eddie, there's no way to stop these

41

stupid, irritating, pernicious boys from calling me Uncle Eddie, it hasn't helped at all that I've repeated time and time again that my name is Edgardo, that they should call me Edgardo because that is my name; it hasn't helped that I ignore them, that I pretend not to have heard when these boys call me Uncle Eddie, they'll never understand that my name is Edgardo, that it's Edgardo and not Uncle Eddie is beyond the reach of their stupid, pernicious little heads that only understand the language of television series, said Vega. Never in my adult life has anyone called me Eddie, Moya, much less Uncle Eddie; if there's anything I detest with intensity it's this horrible custom of diminutives, only vile imbeciles would refer to each other with diminutives, only a vile imbecile would call me Eddie instead of Edgardo, which is what I said to my mother many years ago soon after adolescence, when I had just finished my courses at the school of the Marist Brothers, that's where I knew you, said Vega, and it cost my mother the world to stop calling me Eddie, she understood that my name was Edgardo once I moved to Montreal and two years passed before I said a word to her, I didn't have any communication with her. That's the truth, Moya: stupidity cuts the heart of things in half, it doesn't understand shades of gray, said Vega, which is why I'm content now that I won't have to see or hear my brother's sons anymore, the fact relaxes me that I won't have to hear those irritating boys call me Uncle Eddie, I won't have to respond to their foolish questions about the stupid, pernicious television series that supply their spiritual nourishment, nor will I have to accompany them on outings that only serve to disturb my nerves, said Vega. The worst of all the outings, Moya, the most infamous of these outings, the one that destroyed me almost completely, that left my nerves reduced to dust, was when my brother decided to take me to the port, it was his unfortunate bright idea that we'd go to the sea, to eat seafood and swim together with his wife and his two pernicious kids, because they supposed that a Salvadoran recently returned after many years abroad must long for a trip to the beach and would want to take advantage of the fact that the port is hardly thirty kilometers from San Salvador, my brother imagined that I would return with a robust desire to head to the port, said Vega. A revolting port, Moya; calling a port La Libertad in a country like this can only be the product of a doomed mind, to call a useless and abandoned port La Libertad is more than a joke, calling a ramshackle pier about to crumble into the water La Libertad clearly illustrates these people's concept of liberty, Moya, it's a depressing port, a really horrible place, which is what I said to my brother, how could he consider it a good time to visit a place so depressing, so brutally hot, where the sun beats down with vicious brutality, where the inhabitants typically have the expression of someone who's always brutalized by the heat and sun, said Vega. My brother insisted that we stop at a restaurant called Punta Roca located on the beach some fifty meters from the ramshackle pier, a restaurant whose main attraction is its proximity to the sea and the ramshackle pier, which I tolerated only because it protected me from the brutalizing sun, and there was a breeze that hardly made a dent in that dense, brutal heat, said Vega. Once settled at the restaurant, Moya, with the pernicious boys ruining everything, my brother invited me to eat a conch cocktail, he said there wasn't a greater joy than returning to this country to enjoy a conch cocktail and an ice-cold Pilsener, he said this to me, Moya, as if I hadn't told him that this revolting beer gave me diarrhea, as if I hadn't said that I didn't have any desire to eat conch, for the clean and simple reason that it revolted me, there's nothing more repugnant than those mollusks twisting under lime juice, Moya, it seemed to me inconceivable that someone could eat something so revolting, Moya, only one time did I try those creatures more than twenty years ago, and that was enough to confirm that these filthy creatures tasted like excrement, nothing seems more like eating excrement than eating conch, Moya, the taste of it I uniquely associate with the taste of excrement, it's something nauseating, a truly nauseating act that could only occur to people brutalized by the heat and sun of the coast, which is what I said to my brother, that I didn't have the least interest in eating something as nauseating as a conch cocktail, that for nothing in the world would I decide to put in my mouth a living creature that tasted like excrement, said Vega. My brother got especially annoying, Moya, because I told him that conch seemed to me more nauseating than pupusas, that conch and pupusas were the typical snacks of this country only confirmed my idea that the people here have dull palates. You can't imagine how I suffered on this outing, Moya, you can't imagine the grade of desperation that came on thanks to the sultry brutalizing sun and heat, nor can you imagine the level of my nervous irritation at this port under the brutal sun and heat, nor the agitation I suffered in this restaurant accosted by those pernicious kids and the presence of my brother chewing these nauseating conches with their taste of excrement and the sight of the ramshackle pier there in the distance, said Vega. The worst was when my brother proposed we take a dip, he said it like that, we should take a dip now that the tide was low, jumping into the sea would reanimate me, the force of the waves would do me good, there's nothing more healthy than bathing in the sea under the sun; he would lend me a bathing suit, it would cheer me up, is how he said it. It's incredible, Moya, that my brother thought that I could be ridiculed in this way, said Vega, that I could feel pleasure going out almost nude under the brutal sun and cover myself with dirty sand and salt water, that I would enthusiastically go out and roll around in the waves and the filthy sand. I've never seen more horrible beaches than those in this country, Moya, I've never seen dirtier sand than on these beaches, and the port of La Libertad without a single doubt has the most abominable beaches with sand so filthy, one would need to be exceptionally shameless to roll around in it, only the most shameless could feel some pleasure rolling around in the filthy sand of these abominable beaches, which is what

I said to my brother, that for nothing in the world would I go out and brutalize myself under this sun, and cover myself in filthy sand, stay there sticky with the malodorous water of this abominable beach, said Vega. Now I'm calm because I won't have any more of these outings, Moya, my brother won't have the audacity to invite me on an outing again, to invite me to return to those places that Salvadorans living abroad miss with a feeling that reveals their congenital stupidity, although to tell the truth the primary instigator of these outings was my brother's wife, Clara, about whom I haven't said anything to you, Moya, nothing is more repulsive to describe than this human being, this is the first time I encountered someone of such a nature, a freak whose entire intellect is limited to the newspaper's society pages and Mexican soap operas, an ex-employee of a chain of clothing stores, no one knows how she hooked my madman of a brother and convinced him to fund this gruesome thing she calls a home, said Vega. You wouldn't believe it, Moya, how this freak rummages through the society pages of the newspapers, spends every morning of every day microscopically combing the society pages of those newspapers with extreme emotion; it's her principal entertainment, the only thing that gives meaning to her life: knowing about tea parties, birthdays and anniversaries, engagements and weddings, the births and deaths of people whom she will never know, because she was only a clerk at a chain of clothing stores lucky enough to meet a lunatic dedicated to keys and locks, said Vega. It's incredible, Moya, this little ex-clerk spends all her time talking about society events, knows each and every thing about the society people, she passionately enjoys what happens to them thanks to meticulously memorizing the newspaper society pages. I've never seen a freak of this nature before, Moya, I swear to you, I never imagined I'd encounter someone whose greatest ambition in life is to appear in the newspaper's society pages, I never imagined someone who called me *brother-in-law* would a second later want to relate to me the most recent gossip about people she knows only from the society pages in the newspapers, said Vega. A vomitous freak, Moya, a little ex-clerk who could only ever appear in these society pages with great difficulty, undoubtedly she'll never meet the society people she reads about with so much excitement, because society people aren't interested in meeting little ex-clerk social climbers, especially some freak who spends the morning with her head filled with curlers, the television on, and her attention glued to gossip about society people in the newspapers, said Vega. You'd have to see her, Moya, with her head filled with curlers and the television at top volume as she feverishly combs the newspaper society pages, it's a grotesque spectacle, a vomitous aberration, said Vega. And in the afternoons it's worse: she sits in front of the television to watch those worthless Mexican soap operas, all afternoon she spends in front of the television moved by these worthless stupid Mexican soap operas, while simultaneously gossiping on the phone with her friends about people she's read about in the society pages and about the Mexican soap operas currently intoxicating her, she spends her life chattering on the phone with friends who are surely, or have been, clerks at the same chain of clothing stores where she worked and who also dream of appearing in the newspaper society pages and personally knowing people whose gossip they continually read about, little clerks, or little clothing-store ex-clerks, who live as if life were a Mexican soap opera, as if *they* were the frivolous, stupid actresses starring in these worthless Mexican soap operas, said Vega. My brother's wife is truly a nutcase, Moya, a nutcase right out of the Mexican soap operas, a freak who makes me surprised at my capacity to endure fifteen days in that house, which was a feat for me, although it cost me my health, although it cost me the exacerbation of my colitis and was a shock to my nervous system, truly it was a feat for me. But order another whisky, Moya, don't wait for me, said Vega, I can only handle two drinks, not more, thanks to my colitis; here's what I do, Moya: I drink two whiskeys and later I stick with pure mineral water, because although I know I can only handle two drinks and I can't have one more thanks to my nervous colitis, I drink them hurriedly like I have today, every day it's the same, I can't help it, I drink my pair of whiskeys rapidly, and later I stick to drinking pure mineral water, said Vega, because at the end of the day what I most enjoy is calmly spending a couple of hours, without those annoying drunks from the bars, where they drink that appalling diarrhea-inducing beer; I enjoy listening to the music that I like, thanks to Tolín who satisfies my requests at this hour when he hardly ever has anyone else here. I enjoy the dusk, Moya, I love savoring the dusk from this patio, it's the only thing that calms me, the only thing that relaxes me in this city made especially to irritate my nerves, on this patio I get refreshed, Moya, under these mango and avocado trees I take refuge from this stiflingly hot city, this has been my oasis to flee my absurd agitation and the stupidity of my brother and his Mexican soap-opera freak and their pernicious kids. I'm lucky now that I can pass the time locked in my hotel room reading the books I brought from Montreal, said Vega, I had the foresight to bring with me enough books to avoid sinking into the most profound desperation, I foresaw that in this country I wouldn't encounter anything to nourish my spirit: no books, no art exhibitions, no theatrical productions, no films, absolutely nothing to nourish my spirit, Moya, here they confound vulgarity with art, they confound stupidity and ignorance with art, I don't believe there exists a place more at odds with art and manifestations of the spirit, you only need to stay in this bar until after eight at night, when the so-called artistic events begin, to realize that they confound art with imitation here. I don't believe there exists another place with its creative energies so sapped when it comes to anything related to art and manifestations of the spirit, said Vega. The first day I came to this bar I stayed until late at night, Moya, to be present for the "artistic event": a group of kids came to the stage in front of the bar, one of the country's leading rock groups, that's what the poster said. It was an excruciating experience, Moya, an overwhelming form of terrorizing anyone with the least bit of artistic sensibility, the most grotesque form I have encountered of confounding noise with music; nothing interested these heartlessly out-of-tune guys except their music, they exalted in their vile imitation of old songs by English rock groups, shamelessly destroying songs by the Beatles, the Rolling Stones, and Led Zeppelin; I never saw anyone so shamelessly and despicably destroy the music of those old English groups, Moya, I left terrified, with my nerves fried. The following day, Tolín asked me if I planned to stay for the "artistic event" that night, when they would present a Latin American folk-music group. I responded no, for nothing in the world would I return for that experience, said Vega, Latin American folk music I find especially detestable, Moya, especially repugnant, I've always hated Latin American folk music, there's nothing worse than weepy music from the Andes interpreted by guys dressed in Andean ponchos, guys who consider themselves champions of good causes because they interpret this weepy music disguised in Andean ponchos, they're actually deceitful people disguising themselves as genuine Latin Americans, they sweet talk imbeciles who feel as if they're involved in a good cause by listening to this weepy music. I know very well these deceitful people dedicated to profiting from this detestable and weepy Latin American folk music, I know very well this ilk because in Montreal they band together in such a revolting way, Moya, for decades the Latin American has been identified with this detestable music made fashionable by Chilean communists who were expelled by Pinochet. I fled from leftist Salvadorans with as much repugnancy as I did from the Chilean communists guilty of popularizing this weepy, detestable music, Moya. The worst thing that could ever happen to me would be to come from Montreal to San Salvador to hear that detestable music interpreted by guys disguising themselves as Latin Americans, which is what I said to Tolín, said Vega. Once was enough to cure me of any interest in this so-called artistic event that they present at this bar, the vile rock group was enough. Leafing through newspapers and watching television in my brother's house has been enough to give me an idea of the wasteland I'm in, Moya, it's a pit, a super-deep well, and the self-proclaimed artists and their works are nothing more than something of a pathetic farce: they believe in ideals, but their ignorance and mediocrity are such that they believe they are ideal artists. But they're vulgar, mediocre simulators, Moya. It's truly revolting, said Vega, this country where there are no artists, only simulators, where the only creators are half-assed imitators. I don't know what you're doing here, Moya, if you're dedicating yourself to literature, as you say, you ought to look elsewhere. This country is nowhere, I can assure you as someone who was born here, I regularly receive the world's leading art periodicals, I read with care the sections on culture and art in the world's leading newspapers and magazines, which is why I can assure you that this country is nothing, at least artistically, no one knows anything about it, it interests no one, no one born here matters in the world of art because the world of art is not the world of politics or crime, said Vega. You've got to get yourself out of here, Moya, set sail, relocate to a country that exists, it's the only way you'll write something worthwhile, instead of your famished little stories they publish and applaud you for, that's good for nothing, Moya, pure provincial groveling, you need to write something worth it, and here you won't do it, I'm sure. I've already told you: this place is at odds with art and any manifestation of the spirit; its only vocation is commerce and business, which is why everyone wants to be a business administrator, to better manage their commercial and business dealings, this is why everyone bows at the feet of the military, because they learned to be effective businessmen and establish business connections with them from the beginning thanks to the war, said Vega. It's an illiterate culture, Moya, a culture that denies itself the written word, without any vocation of record or historical memory, without any perception of the past, it's a "gadfly culture" whose only horizon is the present, the immediate, a culture with the memory of a gadfly, crashing every two seconds against the same window glass because after two seconds it's already forgotten that the glass existed. It is a miserable culture, Moya, for which the written word doesn't have the least importance, it jumped from the most atrocious illiteracy to fascinate itself with the stupidity of television, a fatal jump, Moya, this culture, jumping over the written word, cleanly and simply sailing above the centuries in which humanity developed thanks to the written word, said Vega. But the truth is, Moya, beyond this cultural misery, since I feel affection for you, I'll tell you what you should value if you really want to be a writer: if you really have talent, the will, and the discipline required to create a work of art, I say this to you seriously, Moya, with your famished little stories you're not going to go anywhere, it's not possible at your age to continue publishing your famished little stories that go absolutely unnoticed, that no one knows or reads, your famished little stories don't exist, Moya, only for your neighborhood friends. Those famished little stories about sex and violence aren't worth it, I say this to you with affection, Moya, you'd be better off staying in journalism or in another discipline; but at your age, to be publishing these famished stories is a pity, said Vega, no matter how much sex and violence you put into them, there's no way these famished little stories will transcend. Don't waste your time, Moya, this isn't a country of writers, it's impossible for this country to produce writers of quality; it's not possible for writers who are worth it to emerge in this country where no one is interested in literature, art, or any manifestation of the spirit. Just look at the well-known cases, the provincial legends, and you'll see that they're about average writers, without universal appeal, always more preoccupied with ideology than literature; you don't have to wear yourself out, Moya, just compare this country's writers with those of neighboring countries and you realize that the local legends are second-rate: Salarrué, unlike Asturias, is more interested in these backwaters, in outdated esoterics, than literature, he dedicated himself more to becoming a saint of the people than writing a vast and universal work; Roque Dalton, as opposed to Rubén Darío, seems like a fanatical communist whose best attribute was being assassinated by his own comrades, a fanatical communist who wrote some decent poetry, but who, in his ideological obstinacy, wrote the most shameful, hair-raisingly horrible pro-communist poems, a fanatic and crusader for communism whose life and work was more enthusiastically kneeled before than Castro's; for him, the ideal society was a dictatorship like Castro's, Dalton was a blockhead who died in his fight to establish a government like Castro's in these lands, assassinated by his own comrades who until then were Castro supporters, said Vega. It's truly sad, Moya, truly a calamity, proof that the disgrace in which these people live contaminates even their best minds with ideological fanaticism, irrefutable proof that ideological fanaticism belongs to those living in disgrace. Now night is falling, Moya, the best hour of the day if it weren't for these miserable mosquitoes that will soon appear to make our lives miserable, these miserable mosquitoes haven't let me be since I came to this country, Moya, there hasn't been a night in which a squadron of miserable mosquitoes hasn't come to wake me up and fry my nerves, nothing has fried my nerves more than being woken up in the middle of the night by these miserable mosquitoes with their desperate hum, their insidious, desperate hum that's turned all of my nights since I returned to this country into a nightmare, Moya, there hasn't been a night in which I haven't had to wake up and turn on the bedroom light in my brother's house to defend myself against these miserable mosquitoes, capable of frying my nerves with their insidious, desperate hum like nothing else I've ever experienced, said Vega. I'm tremendously anxious to know if in the hotel room, as in the room in my brother's house, a squadron of mosquitoes will also appear in the middle of the night to disrupt my dreams, to fry my nerves, to force me to turn on the lights and put me in a state of alert to detect their hum and then attack them with my open palm. Although in my brother's house, I'm sure the mosquitoes got in because the servant never followed my instructions to close the door and windows of my room after six in the evening, she was sluggish and destructive and never complied with this or any other instruction I gave her: she was a busty, potbellied, hugely backsided woman capable of destroying whatever garment or object fell into her hands, a sluggish destructive automaton who tore the buttons off most of my shirts and stained a few other of my favorite garments, ironing my pants in such a way that I wouldn't be able to wear them again without blushing. What a disgraceful human being, Moya, this sluggish servant of my brother; Tina is what they call her, someone who although she wears a uniform every time, after she says goodbye she is a filthy, stinking, petty little thief, she forced me to always take my valuables with me, a filthy deformity, who always kept part of the change when I sent her to buy something from the store, a potbellied woman whose legs are covered in welts from mosquito bites, she has a pudgy face showing all the tortillas and fat she stuffs herself with; she's a woman who is always chewing a tortilla, Moya; she couldn't live if she didn't have a piece of tortilla in her snout: a true slug, she is a species of animal compatible only with my brother's wife. That deformity and that freak make a hair-raising pair, said Vega. And more surprising, Moya, what left me with my mouth hanging open, what was inconceivable, was my brother's comment that this potbellied slug had "nice legs," that's what he said when she left for the night, Moya, almost with excitement, that her filthy legs covered in welts and with muck lodged in the pores were "nice legs"—can you imagine?—those legs deformed by welts and filth seemed to my brother like "nice legs." It's enough to make you vomit, Moya, to ask what the hell makes the people of this country so dimwitted, with tastes so despicable. I don't have the least doubt that all the experiences I've lived these past fifteen days could be synthesized into a single phrase: *the degradation of taste*. I don't know any culture, Moya— hear me well and consider that my specialty consists of studying cultures—I don't know any culture like this that has been carried to such levels of degraded taste, I don't know any other culture that has made the degradation of taste a virtue, no culture in contemporary history has made the degradation of taste its ideal, its most prized virtue, said Vega. You can see it the moment you board the plane to come here. It's a trip I don't recommend to anyone suffering from a nervous condition; just making the trip disturbs the nerves, Moya; it is a trip that after a while drove me to an uncontrollable nervous crisis. I've never had a similar experience, Moya. I boarded the plane in New York after hurriedly traveling from Montreal, without imagining that when we stopped in Washington the aircraft would fill with louts with criminal faces shadowed by their sombreros, these men wearing sombreros with criminals faces fortunately had been disarmed of machetes and daggers by security; some daggers I'm sure made it through, though without security I'm sure they would have been armed with a butcher's shop of machetes inside that aircraft. You have no idea what happened on this trip, Moya. They assigned me a middle seat between one of these men in a sombrero and some chubby woman in an apron, said Vega, a man in a sombrero who compulsively picked his nose, smearing his snot wherever he could, and this chubby woman who sweated profusely, wiping her sweat with her apron or with a towel that she carried rolled around her neck. During takeoff they maintained their distance: Fuckface in the sombrero enraptured by his snot and Fatty squeezing out her towel. It was the only moment of tranquility I had on the flight, the only moment of peace and quiet, Moya, because once we were in the air, with the plane at cruising altitude and the stewardesses serving the first round of drinks, my companions in the seats on either side started talking to me at almost the same time, shouting more than talking, first with me and later between themselves and then again with me; they practically drenched me in saliva, Moya, jabbing me with their elbows, in a sort of hysterical confession about what had happened to them during their last few years in Washington, a hysterical confession of incidents in the lives of two Salvadoran immigrants in Washington, the *adventures* of Fuckface in the sombrero, who didn't stop compulsively picking his nose, and Fatty, who occasionally rubbed me with her nasty towel soaked with her no less filthy sweat. It was horrible, Moya, because the more they spoke, the more their enthusiasm grew, and the more intensely they exuded their putrid odors, ceaselessly relating to me incidents and adventures I didn't have the least interest in hearing, said Vega. It was a macabre preamble of what waited for me once I arrived in San Salvador, a hair-raising voyage in which Fuckface in the sombrero vociferously told me he was headed to a tiny little town called Polorós, he'd worked as a gardener in Washington and it had been three years since he had returned to El Salvador, meanwhile Fatty replied that she was from Osicala, that she worked as a maid in Washington and hadn't returned to El Salvador in five years. The worst was when they were served the first drink, Moya, never have I seen people so easily lose their grip, I've never seen people go so crazy without warning after one drink: they started to spit on the floor of the cabin, not stopping their shouting, spitting and accompanying their shouts with the most obscene gestures, with the most obscene laughter; meanwhile Fuckface in the sombrero shamelessly smeared his boogers even on the little window and Fatty brandished her towel like an assault weapon. There was a moment in which I thought my nerves would explode, said Vega, and so I stood up to go to the bathroom; then I discovered that scenes similar to the one occurring in my row were taking place in most parts of the cabin. It was horrible, Moya, a horrific experience, the worst flight of my life, seven hours passed in that cabin replete with men wearing sombreros who seemed recently escaped from some insane asylum, seven hours stuck between drooling characters shouting and crying in gibberish because they were about to return to this pit, seven hours, between people completely smashed with alcohol, anticipating the imminent arrival at their so-called homeland. I swear, Moya, I've never even seen a scene in a film similar to this, in no novel have I read anything like this flight spent sitting between these lunatics, their lunacy exacerbated by a couple of drinks and proximity to their birthplace, said Vega. It was truly hair-raising, a spectacle I could only escape for a few moments when I took refuge in the bathroom, but soon enough the bathrooms turned revolting thanks to spit, the vomit, urine, and other excretions; soon enough the bathrooms became unbreathable spaces because people urinated in the sinks, Moya, I'm sure these drooling men in sombreros with their criminal looks, excited about their imminent return to this filthy pit of a country, urinated in the sinks, only that they urinated in the sinks could explain the stench that soon made it impossible for me to take refuge in the bathrooms. And that's not all, Moya, I still can't believe the instant that the sweaty, chubby woman, with her towel rolled around her neck and her apron in disarray, stood up, spat on the floor, and began to shriek, shaking her glass in a way that splashed me with liquor, shouting that some atrocious liquor called Muñeco was ten times better than this whisky, rabidly insisting that the atrocious liquor Muñeco, which is better suited to combat foot fungus, was much better than the so-called faggy whisky they were drinking, she was insulting the stewardesses because they would no longer serve her another shot of this "faggy" whisky; and suddenly Fatty, who every second sweated more copiously and now threateningly brandished her soaked towel, looked like someone who was about to vomit, said Vega. She left in a huge rush, and I took refuge in the extra cargo compartment next to the bathroom entrance, with my nerves on end, ranting against the fact that my mother had died the day before and I was obliged to return to a country I detested above all else, a country inhabited by drooling freaks with criminal features accustomed to urinating in the sinks of airplanes in flight, inhabited by sweating fat women gone mad who waited for the least provocation to throw up all over their neighbors in airplanes in flight. You can imagine, Moya, that I left the plane in an absolutely disturbed state, it had been my sea-son in hell; reaching the airport corridors had become my greatest desire for the last few hours, the arrival at Comalapa Airport was my salvation, the possibility of returning to some semblance of normalcy, the possibility of reaching somewhere else, someplace different from those seven hours locked in an airplane cabin with sinister beings who smeared boogers on the little windows or tried to shake out a towel drenched in sweat, said Vega. Imagine my surprise, Moya, when upon arriving at immigration I found myself among hundreds of similar individuals to those who were on my plane, that I encountered furious masses exactly like those on my flight, hundreds of men wearing sombreros and chubby women with aprons arriving from Los Angeles, San Francisco, Houston, and who knows what other cities, an immense swirling throng that turned immigration into overwhelming chaos. I was worried I would break down at any moment, said Vega, which is why I tried to leave that ball of confusion, I made my best effort to open a path through these sinister masses, concentrating all my energy to open a path through the asphyxiating masses and arrive at a bathroom where I could take refuge, where I could gather my forces, and so for half an hour I locked myself in a toilet stall, victim of an attack of distress, to the point of shattering, sweating out the shakes, saying there was no turning back, I was already in this place in which I had sworn I would never set foot again. I still feel chills down my spine just remembering it, Moya. I left the toilet stall exhausted, washed my face in the sink, frenetically rubbed my face in front of the mirror, convincing myself that things wouldn't be so totally horrible, repeating to myself that I came only for my mother's funeral, to take the steps necessary to qualify for my share of the inheritance, that there was nothing to fear because I was a Canadian citizen, my passport was with me in my jacket pocket, my best protection against all of this. I supposed that the crowd had by now been removed from immigration, said Vega, so I made one last effort to confront the immigration official, a brown and blubber-lipped dwarf, who took my passport without even looking at me, consulted his computer, stamped the country's seal, and said "Pass." But I wasn't fated to free myself so easily from that throng of men in sombreros and chubby ladies. I saw going down the escalator toward customs—it was horrible, Moya—that here was the same pandemonium I'd encountered in immigration, and worse still, hundreds of individuals swirled between the walls and the conveyor belts where the luggage emerged, hundreds of individuals feverishly throwing elbows and spitting wads as they grabbed their enormous boxes filled with the most random merchandise, hundreds of people gone mad accumulating more and more boxes as though this baggage pickup area were a chaotic and asphyxiating market. I don't know how I managed to rescue my suitcase, Moya, but it didn't matter, because I had to wait hours until every one of these characters with their dozens of boxes passed the minutest possible inspection by the customs official, a vermin with glasses and a mustache who managed to entertain himself for the longest possible time inspecting every box, a vermin whose mission was to raise everyone's feverishness to delirious levels, who evidently took pleasure in increasing the stress of those hundreds of people anxious for their boxes replete with the most useless crap to pass as quickly as possible through inspection, these people had done thankless or ignominious jobs over the past few years to save the money that would let them buy these enormous quantities of crap to bring as gifts to their relatives, who now waited drooling and greedy on the other side of the glass door, said Vega. And when at last I managed to pass through this glass door leading to the street, I came out on top of another sticky throng, a hair-raising mass of people in whose faces only the desire for grabbing these boxes shone, these boxes filled with useless crap. The tropics are horrific, Moya, they convert men into putrid beings who live by their most basic instincts, like those people against whom I was forced to rub up against leaving the terminal area to look for a taxi. No experience is more abhorrent than leaving the Comalapa Airport, Moya, no experience has made me hate these tropics with such intensity as the departure from the terminal area of the Comalapa Airport: it's not just the multitudes, Moya, it's the shock of passing from a bearable climate inside the airport to this blistering, brutal hell of the tropical coast, the withering breath of heat that transformed me in an instant to a sweaty animal. Once

I managed to open a path through the masses, drooling with greed before their boxes of useless crap, I was suddenly assaulted by a flock of taxi drivers, who marked their territory with shoves, fighting over me like vultures, uniformed taxi drivers with sky-blue guayaberas and dark sunglasses trying to snatch my suitcase, said Vega. I'd never seen guys whose faces were so clearly marked with betrayal, Moya, I'd never seen faces so grim as those of the taxi drivers. But I had no alternative; the trip was so improvised that I hadn't even phoned my brother to inform him what flight I was arriving on. I told the taxi driver to take me to the funeral home, quickly, my mother had died the day before, they were waiting for me before they buried her. And as he traveled the forty kilometers separating San Salvador from Comalapa Airport, the way that the wind entered the window allowed me to compose myself and attain a certain peace of mind; I had a hint of a certain definition that in these fifteen days I have been able to fully confirm: the Salvadoran is the *cuilio* everyone carries inside him. My taxi driver was the perfect example: he intended to draw from me as much information as he possibly could, asking malicious questions that made me afraid that he was weighing whether it was worth it to assault me or not, said Vega. At the least opportunity, a cop will show his vocation for petty thievery, true petty thieves work as cops, only in this country do they use the word *cuilio* to denote a petty thief working as a policeman, but in this case a taxi driver snoop was asking me all these questions about my life in order to determine if I were a favorable victim upon whom it would be worth exercising his vocation for petty thievery. All taxi drivers are *cuilios*, Moya, especially that one who drove me to San Salvador and asked suspicious questions about my life. At the entrance of the city, before the toll booth, the taxi driver told me that now there was this "Monument to Peace," a grotesquerie that could only have been conceived by someone with a screwed-up imagination, a grotesque "Monument to Peace" showing the absolute lack of imagination of these people, forceful evidence of the total degradation of taste, said Vega. And the one further on is even worse, Moya, it's the most hair-raising thing I have ever seen; the so-called Monument to the Distant Brother actually seems like a gigantic urinal, this monument with its enormous wall of tiles doesn't evoke anything other than a urinal, I swear to you, Moya, when I saw it for the first time I didn't feel anything other than an urge to urinate, and every time I've passed by this place they decided to call "Monument to the Distant Brother," the only thing it has done is excite my kidneys. It's a masterpiece of the degradation of taste: a gigantic urinal constructed in appreciation of men in sombreros and chubby women who live in the United States loaded down with boxes replete with useless crap, said Vega. Only a party of idiots could be so obsessed to construct this hair-raising monument, Moya, only a bunch of idiots who've become the governing party could waste state funds on the construction of these failures, starkly expressing this country's degraded taste, only a party of idiots enjoying the use of state funds could foment such a degradation of taste by constructing these so-called monuments. They are, truthfully, monuments to the degradation of taste, Moya, they are nothing more than monuments to the lack of imagination, the extreme degradation of taste of the people in this country, said Vega. And what can I say about the enormous heads of the so-called Heroes of the Fatherland, these enormous, deformed heads of marble placed at a distance from what was once called the Southern Highway, these horrendous unwieldy monstrosities of marble supposedly reproducing the so-called heroes of the fatherland's faces, these horrendous and deformed heads popularly known as "The Flintstones": only a caveman mentality could have conceived such unwieldy monstrosities, Moya, only a comic-strip, caveman mentality could have conceived of these hulks as sculptures to be exhibited publicly, something that in another place would have been considered with horror, here they exhibit with pride. It's incredible, Moya. They call it "The Flintstones" because the so-called heroes of the fatherland surely weren't anything other than cavemen, like the idiots now wasting state funds by ordering the construction of monuments and sculptures that only serve to reveal their total degradation of taste, said Vega; the so-called heroes of the fatherland had to have been cavemen, and from them was passed down the congenital imbecility that's characterized the people of this country, only the fact that the so-called heroes of the fatherland were cavemen could explain the general monstrous-

66

ness prevailing in this country. Let me buy you one last whisky, Moya, offered Vega, one more before you leave, while I drink my last mineral water, and I'll ask Tolín to return my CD of Tchaikovsky's Piano Concerto in B-flat Minor, because people have already begun to arrive: the clientele who have surely come to reserve tables for the so-called artistic event tonight. By seven I want to be back at my hotel, to lock myself in to enjoy my room and a frugal dinner, said Vega. Nothing's more pleasant than lying in bed, calmly reading, without the sound of televisions nearby, without the enervating shouts of my brother's wife and their pernicious children; there's nothing more comforting than locking myself in to read, think, and rest. Just the idea of being safe from my brother's nightly invitations to "go party" I find stimulating, Moya, nothing's more horrible than being forced to choose between my brother's invitations to "go party" and the prospect of spending the night flanked by three television sets cranked to top volume on different channels. Only one night did I accept my brother's invitation to "go party," said Vega, a unique unrepeatable night that I spent so that it would never again occur to me to accept my brother's repeated invitation to "go party." My brother's primary pleasure is to "go party" at night, Moya, he and his friends' primary pleasure consists of hanging out in a bar drinking huge quantities of diarrhea-inducing beer until they reach complete imbecility; later they enter a discotheque where they jump around like primates; and, finally, they visit a sordid brothel. These are the three stages of "partying" at night, this ritual they maintain with gusto, it's their supreme diversion: first they dumb themselves all the way down with beer, then they jump around sweating to savage noise in the thick air of a discotheque, and finally they drool with lust in a seedy brothel, said Vega. At least these were the three rigorous stages of partying on the night my brother took me with them. Only the disturbance produced in me by the noise of the television sets, by the chitchat of my brother's wife, and by the shouts of the pair of stupid, pernicious boys could explain why I accepted my brother's invitation to "go party" that night, knowing all along that no invitation coming from my brother would lack a disturbing vulgarity. I will repent for the rest of my life having accepted this invitation to "go party" that night, Moya, I suffered the worst anxiety imaginable, I wasted practically all my emotional capital, said Vega. It was my brother, a friend of his called Juancho, and me. First we were at a bar called The Barbed-Wire Fence, a lurid place, enough to make your hair stand on end, it's a shack plagued with gigantic screens in every corner, truly an aberration: a place where you can only drink diarrhea-inducing beer surrounded by screens on which different singers are projected, each singer more abominable than the last, interpreting those foolish and strident melodies. And my brother's friend, Moya, this Juancho, a guy with negroid features, talked up a storm; he's a negroid who owns a hardware store, he swears to have downed all the alcohol in the world and gone to bed with every woman who ever crossed his path, said Vega. El Negroid exaggerated more and was more mythomaniacal than you could imagine, Moya, a machine of talking and telling stories about himself, a talking doll who drinks beer after beer while narrating about his delirious sexual prowess. I wasn't prepared for this: stuck with my glass of mineral water, I was forced to listen with one ear to the verbosity of El Negroid and with the other to the strident voice of some disheveled girl gyrating on the screens. But El Negroid imposed himself against their wailing and as he drank more beer, his stories about his drinking binges and sexual adventures became more and more obscene. A really repulsive negroid, Moya. And foolish like few are: time and again he insisted that I should drink a beer, that it wasn't possible to spend the whole night drinking mineral water. I don't know how many times I explained that I don't drink beer, Moya, much less this revolting, diarrhea-inducing Pilsener they drink, my colitis only permitted me to have a couple of drinks, preferably whisky, but in this bar called The Barbed-Wire Fence they didn't sell anything other than this revolting, diarrhea-inducing beer. In El Negroid's peanut brain, in the center of his little head, there wasn't room for the idea that someone might not drink that filth, said Vega. It was repulsive, Moya, once again he told me his delirious sexual adventures with all the prostitutes in all the brothels in San Salvador. But what truly preoccupied me, Moya, were the four guys at the next table, they were the most sinister people I've ever seen in my life, Moya, four psychopaths with crime and torture stamped on their faces drinking beer at the next table, these were guys you really need to be careful of, so bloodthirsty it seemed that to turn to look at them for just a second constitutes a tremendous risk, said Vega. I warned El Negroid to lower his voice, that these lovely guys to the side were already watching him with creepy grins. I feared a tragedy, Moya, these psychopaths evidently carried fragmentation grenades they anxiously hoped to throw under the table of a trio of guys like us, I was sure at this instant that these criminals stroked fragmentation grenades that at any moment they would throw under our table, because for these psychopath ex-soldiers, ex-guerillas, fragmentation grenades have become their favorite toys, not a day passes in which one of these so-called demobilized guys doesn't throw a frag grenade at a group of people bothering him, truthfully these criminal ex-soldiers and ex-guerrillas really carry fragmentation grenades hoping for the least opportunity to throw them at guys like El Negroid who wouldn't stop shouting about his most unusual sexual adventures, said Vega. I warned him time and time again to lower his voice, Moya, and he calmed down for a second, whirling to look at these psychopaths about to throw fragmentation grenades at us the way they do every day in bars and dance halls, and in the streets, where they settle their differences with grenades, like kids, where these so-called demobilized guys have fun with their fragmentation grenades, throwing them while laughing at imbeciles like El Negroid, said Vega. Luckily we rushed out of the bar for a discotheque called

Rococó, in the second stage of what my brother and his friends denoted "partying." It was a dark hall, with blinding lights pulsing vividly from the ceiling and where the air hardly circulated, a hall that thumped with infernal noise and in the center of which there was a dance floor surrounded by seats and tables practically encrusted to the floor. An overwhelming place, Moya, especially made for the deranged and deaf who enjoy darkness and dense air. I immediately began to sweat, to feel my temples palpitate as if my blood pressure had increased out of control and my head were about to burst, said Vega. And after we made it to the bar to order the drink that came with the cover charge, in the middle of a desperate scramble, while we looked for a table, I realized that El Negroid hadn't stopped talking for a single minute, that his voice strenuously fought to be heard over the shocking noise threatening to demolish the hall. I drank my shot of whisky, hoping it might help ease my palpating head, but it only served to make me sweat more profusely, accentuating my sensation of claustrophobia. I can't stand these enclosed, dark, noisy, asphyxiating places, Moya, and least of all next to El Negroid almost shouting as he repeated the same story about his extraordinary sexual adventures, said Vega. My resistance to nervousness was giving in. A dozen pairs of people jumped around on the dance floor and their silhouettes could hardly be distinguished thanks to the extravagant lights and the pulsing, blinding flashes from the ceiling. My brother commented that the discotheque was pretty empty, it wasn't a good night, there were hardly any single girls; El Negroid hurried to recount each and every one of the times he'd picked up goodlooking girls at this place, each and every one of the times that, after dancing at the discotheque, he'd directed them to a motel to make love, to tell the truth every time he'd gone to this discotheque he'd managed to pick up a girl, El Negroid shouted, said Vega. I started to feel dizzy, Moya, like I needed air, I said this to my brother, that I was feeling sort of bad, that this place wasn't doing anything good for me, it'd be better if we went somewhere that wasn't so distressing. I had to shout so my brother would hear me, I almost tore out my throat to make myself heard between the thumping, deafening noise and El Negroid's shouts. My brother asked me to hold on a while, to see if more girls showed up, it'd be a waste to leave the discotheque so early, he said, but I was becoming despondent, I feared that at any moment everything would start to spin on me and I'd suffer a breakdown, so I told my brother not to worry, I'd head home in a taxi, El Negroid and he could stay as late as they wanted. So then my brother came out and said that I couldn't abandon them like that, that's what he said, Moya, "abandon them," that if I arrived home alone, his wife would suspect the worst, that I should wait for them for no more than five minutes, I could go rest for a while in the car, and then we'd visit a less claustrophobic place. And so I did, Vega said. But when my brother gave me the keys to the car I warned him that I would wait five minutes, not a second more, and that he should remember my profound sense of punctuality, that if he didn't appear exactly in five minutes I would leave the keys with the doorman of the discotheque and take off in a taxi. I hate unpunctual people, Moya, there's nothing worse than unpunctuality, it's impossible to have any sort of dealings with late people, nothing more noxious and irritating than people who are not on time. If you hadn't come at five this evening on the dot, Moya, I assure you I wouldn't have waited for you, although I love being at this place between five and seven in the evening to drink my two whiskeys, but even if I had to sacrifice that moment of calm, I wouldn't have waited for you, because the fact that you were late would have been enough to completely disrupt the possibility of having a constructive chat, Moya, your lateness would have totally changed my perception of you, I would have immediately placed you in the category of the most undesirable people, in the category of unpunctual people, said Vega. So once out of the discotheque, walking along the parking lot in the open air, I felt better, although my bewilderment would take a while to disappear. I got into the car, in the seat next to the driver's seat, put away the key, and leaned the seat back. The discotheque was located almost at the end of Paseo Escalón, in the mall. The issue was that after two minutes had passed and I began to relax thanks to the silence of the parking lot and the panoramic view of the city one has from there, suddenly I suffered an intense anxiety attack, as though I were about to be assaulted, I suffered a shocking attack of anxiety that forced me to get up and

73

head out in search of the thugs who might be preparing to attack me, said Vega, a shocking anxiety attack as though the danger were a few steps away, stalking me, ready to transform itself into thugs plotting to make my brother's car their own, this latest Toyota Corolla model that my brother cared for more than himself. It was a sudden panic, Moya, an absolute panic, paralyzing, because thugs in this country kill even without a motive, for the pure pleasure of the crime, they kill even if you don't resist, even if you give them all they ask for, every day they kill without any other reason than the pleasure of killing, said Vega. This was the case of Mrs. Trabanino, the one always on the news. It was tremendous, Moya: a thug surprised her when she parked in the garage of her house and later forced himself into the living room so he could shoot her in front of her two small daughters. Tremendous, Moya, the thug killed her purely for pleasure in front of her little girls, he didn't rob anything, he only wanted to kill. It was a horrible case, Moya. I wouldn't have paid it so much attention but my brother's wife spent three days just talking about Mrs. Trabanino's case, three days ruining my meals with the same harangues about the assassination of Mrs. Trabanino, three days being outraged and venturing hypotheses about what caused the crime when actually, it turned out that my brother's wife was morbidly fascinated, it turned out Mrs. Trabanino was someone from the newspaper society pages that she rummages through with so much delight; morbid fascination is why this freak my brother married didn't stop talking about the assassination of Mrs. Trabanino; she hasn't stopped being paranoid about the extreme criminality raging in this country, said Vega, which is why the five minutes inside my brother's car seemed to me like an eternity, Moya, the last three minutes of which the panic preying on me was horrific, a trying experience, something I don't wish on anyone: to remain trapped in a Toyota Corolla waiting for a group of thugs to assassinate you before they steal your car, because they can't rob without killing, because to kill is what produces true pleasure in them, not so much to rob, as was demonstrated in the case of Mrs. Trabanino, said Vega; I was about to rush out of the car, such was my panic, to take shelter in the doorway of the discotheque's entrance, but I immediately realized that if I left the car, I ran more of a risk of being riddled with bullets, which is why I remained inside, shivering, with a horrible accelerated heartbeat, crouching in the seat, trying to make myself sleep, counting every second, profoundly hating my brother and El Negroid, the two who were guilty of making me suffer like this, said Vega. What taste the people of this country have for living in fear, Moya, such a morbid taste for living terrorized lives, what a perverted taste for the terror of the war turned into the terror of delinquency these people have, a pathological, morbid vice to make terror their permanent way of life. Luckily my brother and El Negroid soon arrived. They got in the car laughing, saying who knows what about whichever woman, to the point that they dared claim it was my fault that they hadn't been able to pick up a pair of chicks who were entering the discotheque just then. So then we threaded our way toward the third stage of what my brother and his friends called "partying," toward the neighborhood *La Rábida* that twenty years ago was an old middle-class residential zone, an old neighborhood now converted into a red-light district teeming with bars and seedy brothels. My brother and El Negroid were in good shape, happy, with their bellies filled with beer and talking recklessly, both at the same time, and not hearing each other, as though each wanted to demonstrate to himself and to me something about his audacity and virility. But I hardly paid attention, Moya, only realizing that in every phrase they included the word *cerote*, said Vega. Never have I seen people with more excrement in their mouths than in this country, Moya, not in vain is *cerote* the most repeated word in their language, they don't have any other word in their mouths; their vocabulary is limited to this word *cerote* and its derivatives: *ceretísimo, cerotear, cerotada*. It's incredible, Moya, when you look at it from a distance, this word designating a piece of excrement, it's vulgar and revolting, signifying a piece of human excrement that's expelled all at once, this most vile word, signifying *a turd*, is the one my brother and El Negroid had stuck in their mouths, said Vega. I particularly detest that when I met that negroid Juancho he called me *cerote* with familiarity, I especially detested that a negroid hardware-store owner I had just met was repeatedly calling me *cerote*, he called me *cerote* as if I were a piece of human excrement expelled all at

76

once. It's horrible, Moya, only in this country could something like this happen, only here do people think of themselves as pieces of human excrement expelled all at once, which then makes it seem perfectly acceptable for my brother and his negroid hardware-store owner friend to repeatedly, affectionately and familiarly, call me *cerote* after they were buzzed by the diarrhea-inducing beer they compulsively drink, driving us to a brothel to complete the third stage of what they called "partying," said Vega. The brothel was called "The Office," Moya, a favorite dive of my brother and evidence that the guy needs to feel like he's in a workplace to exercise his vulgar diversions, as though the fact of feeling as if he's in an office removes him from his sleaziness. You don't know the nausea I suffered, Moya, when we entered this brothel called The Office, never have I felt nausea to such magnitude; only a brothel like The Office could cause such a forceful contraction, the most abominable nausea I have suffered in my life. I hadn't entered a brothel for twenty-two years, Moya, since we were in the last year of high school, do you remember? It was frightening. The fact of entering a brothel again after so many years dredged up the rudest memories of an experience I thought I had buried, a vile denigrating experience which, with difficulty and after much time, I have managed to get over. Sexual commerce is the most revolting thing that exists, Moya, there is nothing as repugnant as carnal commerce; something like sex that is in itself vicious and prone to misunderstandings reaches abominable depths when mixed with

77

commerce, a practice that consumes the spiritual faculties in the most extreme way. But for my brother and El Negroid it's precisely this spiritual void that makes it so joyful and fun, said Vega. I assure you that just by crossing the threshold of The Office I had to walk with extreme care, Moya, careful not to slip on the hardened semen on the tiles. I'm not lying, Moya, this den reeked of semen, in this den there was semen everywhere: it was stuck to the walls, smeared on the furniture, hardened on the tiles. I felt the most devastating nausea of my life, the most tremendous and horrible nausea I have ever felt I felt there in The Office, that den contaminated by greasy women who moved their purulent bodies down hallways and around sitting rooms, purulent tired women whose stuffed bodies spilled over sofas and chairs with so many various, sweaty odors, Vega said. And there I was, Moya, feeling nauseous vertigo, seated on the edge of a chair, my face contracted in revulsion, trying not to let the semen on the sofas and walls get on me, trying not to slip on the hardened semen on the tiles; meanwhile my brother and El Negroid intimated in the most disgraceful way with a couple of greasy women, who at this point were already saturated in semen and sweat to the point of exhaustion. It was incredible, Moya, my brother and his negroid hardware-store owner friend continued feasting on beer and they were happy to smear themselves in the excretions of these women, bargaining from the bottom in order to obtain the best price for a trip to a putrid bed where they would shake obscenely over these sweaty, greasy women, said Vega. Horrendous, Moya. I had never seen more lamentable women, for whom sordidness was their natural way, greasy, fat women stuffed like pigs with the semen of guys transforming the most intimate and desirable pleasure into revolting commercial filth. It was the saddest brothel you can imagine, Moya, with no sensation prevailing other than sordidness, where neither guffaws nor cooing whispers escaped that sordidness permeating everything, imposed on everything, said Vega. There was a moment, Moya, in which I could no longer contain my nausea, above all when one of these greasy women came over to chat me up, wanting to convince me to buy a piece of her sordid, sweaty meat. I immediately stood, Moya, and went in search of the bathroom, walking with extreme care so as not to slip and fall on the hardened semen on the tiles. And then came the worst, Moya: these were the filthiest bathrooms I've seen in my life, I swear to you, I had never seen filthiness like this concentrated in such a small space, said Vega. I reached to take out my handkerchief to cover my nose, but it was already much too late, Moya, I was concentrating on avoiding falling on a pool of semen and urine, defenselessly, I penetrated this chamber of putrid gases, and when I reached to take out my handkerchief it was already too late. I vomited, Moya, the filthiest vomit of my life, the most sordid and revolting vomiting you can imagine, because I was vomiting over vomit, this brothel was an enormous pile of vomit dotted with semen and urine. It is truly indescribable, Moya, my stomach still stirs from the memory. I left the bathroom, trembling, with the firm decision to immediately abandon this revolting den, not caring what argument my brother and his negroid companion presented, I had made the strict decision to get a taxi and direct it to my brother's house, said Vega. And then came the last straw, the improbable, the event that made me enter a delirious spiral, overcome with the most extreme anxiety you can imagine: my passport, Moya, I'd misplaced my Canadian passport! It wasn't in any of my pockets. This was the worst thing that could have happened to me in my life, misplacing my Canadian passport in a filthy brothel in San Salvador. Terror overwhelmed me, Moya, terror pure and shocking: I saw myself trapped in this city forever, unable to return to Montreal; I saw myself converted again into a Salvadoran with no other option than to vegetate in this pit, said Vega. I had kept my Canadian passport in the pocket of my shirt, I was completely sure, but now it wasn't there. I had pulled it out, Moya, my Canadian passport had fallen out with some brusque movement, I hadn't noticed the moment it had fallen out. It was horrible, Moya, a sinister nightmare; I ran back to the bathroom where I had recently vomited, not caring that I could fall headlong onto the hardened semen on the tiles, not caring about the puddles of urine and vomit or the tremendous stench. But my Canadian passport wasn't there, Moya, and it couldn't possibly have fallen into the toilet without my noticing. I looked carefully between the wads of paper smeared with excrement, between the puddles of urine and vomit, but my Canadian passport was nowhere to be found. I left the bathroom absolutely deranged, Moya, I went to share my disgrace with my brother and El Negroid. I urged them to help me find my Canadian passport. It was essential for us to return that instant to the discotheque and the bar. That passport is my most valuable possession, Moya, there's nothing else I more obsessively care for than my Canadian passport, truthfully my life rests on the fact that I am a Canadian citizen, said Vega. But then the negroid hardware-store owner came out and said that I shouldn't worry so much, my passport was probably in my room in my brother's house, I should relax. I responded to his shouts, Moya, that I wasn't an imbecile, that I wasn't talking to him, I was demanding that my brother forget his fat, greasy, sordid whore and help me recover my Canadian passport. I was out of control, Moya, you should have seen me, my desperation was such that I was about to start grabbing and smacking this pair of imbeciles who undervalued the fact that I had misplaced my passport, said Vega. Finally my brother reacted, Moya, and asked if it hadn't fallen out of my pocket in the bathroom. I responded that I had already carefully looked through the toilet paper smeared with shit and the puddles of vomit, urine, and semen, but my Canadian passport wasn't there. Which is when my brother said we should look inside the car before we headed for the discotheque and the bar. I felt the whole world falling down on me, Moya, Canada doesn't have an ambassador or a consulate in El Salvador. I would have to travel to Guatemala and endure lengthy procedures, and my stay here would become interminable. Cold sweat ran down my spine just thinking about it, Moya. We leapt toward the car to look inside, to beat the carpets and look beneath the seats. I was already in a delirious state, Moya, imagining the worst: my Canadian passport had been lost in the bar or the discotheque and I would have enormous problems obtaining a new document, said Vega. I was sweating, my hands trembling, my hysteria was about to make me burst. I shouted at my brother that my Canadian passport wasn't in the car, we needed to leave immediately for the two other foul dens we'd been to earlier, and my brother told me to leave the searching to him, that I needed to calm down, that I shouldn't worry, we'd soon find it. Such a fool, Moya, asking me to calm down. But I stepped aside and let him search the front of the car, said Vega. I was about to crumble, my nerves couldn't handle any more, I was about to start screaming and kicking because I'd misplaced my Canadian passport thanks to these two dirty imbeciles, my brother and El Negroid, thanks to accepting my brother's invitation to "go party." I was about to shatter into infinite pieces when my brother emerged from the car and released a shout of joy. "I found it!" And there it was, Moya, my brother's hand holding my Canadian passport, my brother's stupid smile beside the hand holding my Canadian passport that had fallen from my pocket, I hadn't noticed when I entered the car to flee the asphyxiating discotheque and the negroid hardware guy making me dizzy with verbosity about his extraordinary sexual adventures, said Vega. I snatched my Canadian passport without saying a word, without so much as turning to look at them, I ran toward a taxi stationed a few meters ahead. I left that place like I was pursued by the devil, Moya. And there was no way to calm myself down until I entered the guest room in my brother's house and got into bed absolutely assured that my Canadian passport was securely tucked under my pillow, said Vega. It was the worst scare of my life, Moya. During the ride in the taxi, I clasped my Canadian passport, leafing through it, confirming that I was the one in the photo: Thomas Bernhard, Canadian citizen born thirty-eight years ago in a filthy town called San Salvador. Because this I haven't told you, Moya, I didn't just change my nationality, I changed my name, said Vega. I'm not called Edgardo Vega there, Moya, an otherwise horrible name that only evokes for me the execrable neighborhood *La Vega*, where they assaulted me when I was an adolescent, an old neighborhood that might not even still exist. My name is Thomas Bernhard, Moya, said Vega, it's a name I took from an Austrian writer I admire and who surely neither you nor the other simulators in this infamous place would recognize.

SAN·PEDRO DE LOS PINOS, MEXICO CITY

DECEMBER 31, 1995 – FEBRUARY 5, 1996

Author's note

ALMOST TWENTY YEARS AGO, in the summer of 1997, I was visiting Guatemala City, staying at the house of a poet friend, when the telephone rang in the small hours of the night. It was my mother, calling from San Salvador: still shocked, she told me she had just received two phone calls. A threatening male voice informed her that they would kill me thanks to a short novel that had been published a week ago. With my mouth dry from rising fear and the certainty that my blood pressure had shot up, I managed to ask if the guy had identified himself. She told me no, he hadn't identified himself, but his threats sounded very serious; she alarmedly asked if thanks to these circumstances I still intended to return to El Salvador in the next few days as I had planned.

The novel that awoke such hate is the one now translated into English. I wrote it in 1996–97, in Mexico City, as an exercise in style: I would pretend to imitate the Austrian writer Thomas Bernhard, as much in his prose based on cadence and repetition as in his themes, which contain a bitter critique of Austria and its culture. With the relish of the resentful getting even, I had fun writing this novel, in which I wanted to demolish the culture and politics of San Salvador, same as Bernhard had done with Salzburg, with the pleasure of diatribe and mimicry. I didn't foresee that reactions, including those of some loved ones, would be so virulent: the wife of a writer friend threw her copy into the street, out of her bathroom window, indignant, thanks to Edgardo Vega's barbaric talk about pupusas, the national dish of El Salvador.

Of course I didn't return to San Salvador. I called some friends of international press agencies to tell them about the threat; there was scant coverage in the national press, although it didn't lack a columnist who claimed I had invented the threats to promote the book and that I wanted to imitate Salman Rushdie. I continued earning a living as a journalist in Guatemala, Mexico, and Spain. A colleague mentioned the possibility that the threats could be related to *Primera Plana*, an ephemeral weekly publication I had edited (1994–95). It was very critical of political forces recently emerged from the civil war, and my colleague ventured that *Revulsion* was the straw that broke the camel's back. But this was nothing peculiar. El Salvador isn't Austria. It is a country where, in 1975, its own leftist comrades assassinated the country's most important poet, Roque Dalton, after accusing him of being a CIA agent. I thought it would be better to go into exile than play the martyr.

It's interesting that *Revulsion* didn't exhaust my luck. Despite the threats and my absence, the little book continued to be published every year in El Salvador by a small and valiant publisher, and thanks to one of those twists of fate it ultimately was taught in the university. Soon various copies left for neighboring countries. On more than one occasion—in some bar in Antigua, Guatemala, or in San José, Costa Rica, or in Mexico City—I was introduced to people who expressed admiration for the book and asked me if I would write a *Revulsion* about their respective countries, so to speak, a novel in the style of Thomas Bernhard that would critically demolish their country's culture. Of course I always excused myself, I told them that I had already done my work, mentioning without breaking into a smile, that some countries would require many more pages to complete their *Revulsion* and I was a writer of short novels.

Two years after the threats, in the summer of 1999, I returned with caution to San Salvador for a few days to see my family and take care of some red tape. In a restaurant I encountered a lawyer, an old acquaintance, who worked for an international human rights organization. "What are you doing here? You want them to kill you?" he asked with a gesture that could have been consternation or black humor. The following day I visited various friends, who to my surprise all told me that I had to write the sequel to *Revulsion*, because the country was worse than ever: the political corruption, the organized crime, the gangs, the loss of the value of life ...

But then I had other literary plans. With *Revulsion*, a fact was reconfirmed: thanks to their work, some writers earn money, others obtain fame, and some writers only make enemies. After the publication of my first novel *The Diaspora* that addressed the rot of the leftist Salvadoran revolutionaries during the civil war, I had become part of this latter group. To tell the truth I was tired of that existence. But as Robert Walser said to his editor Carl Seelig: "You can't confront your own country with impunity." Years later, despite having published many other novels since then, on various topics in which I didn't imitate any writer, and not having written the sequel that some asked me to write, for Salvadorans, I remain uniquely and exclusively the author of *Revulsion*. Like a stigma, the little imitation novel and its aftermath pursue me.